Wicked LOVE

VIGILANTE KINGS BOOK THREE

EVA CHANCE
& HARLOW KING

CHAPTER
ONE

Madelyn

Silence seemed to have settled over the campus. Other students were chatting and laughing as they walked along the paths, but they might as well have been miles away from where I stood with my stepbrother's hand clamped around my arm, his best friends flanking us, and all three of them glaring accusingly at the other guy I was falling for.

Logan's words echoed in my mind, sounding no less ridiculous than when I'd first heard them. *We've found out why we're having so much trouble looking into your dad's murder. Beckett's family is behind it, and he's been covering their tracks all along.*

Beckett was blinking at Logan, his forehead

furrowing. "What the hell are you talking about? I thought Maddie's father died from a sudden disease."

Of course he did. Because that was what I'd told him, back when I'd believed that story was true too.

How could he or his family have anything to do with Dad's death? I wasn't *that* bad a judge of character, was I? Beckett had never seemed anything other than considerate and protective toward me.

Heck, he'd just raced to my rescue over an anxious text message I'd sent him. I hadn't seen the slightest sign that he meant me any harm. If he was mixed up in the murder in any way, wouldn't he be trying to get rid of me, not keep me safe?

Logan scoffed, his brown eyes glinting harshly beneath the rumpled tufts of his chestnut hair. "You can't fool us with that innocent act. We know just how many lies you've been peddling."

"This doesn't make any sense," I burst out, spinning to face the Vigil guys. "I know you weren't totally sure about Beckett, but you can't just go around making up crazy stories—"

"It's not crazy, and it's not just a made-up story," Dexter said in his usual matter-of-fact tone, folding his arms over his lean chest and fixing his bright green gaze on Beckett. "We have photographic evidence that he's been hiding things."

Slade looped one of his well-muscled arms around mine—the one Logan didn't still have in a death-grip. An angry flush darkened his bronze skin. "Don't worry,

Piccolina. We'll make sure he gets what he deserves—and that he doesn't set foot anywhere near *you* again."

Beckett ran a hand over the smooth strands of his sandy blond hair, his gray eyes stormy with what still looked like genuine confusion to me, along with a fair bit of frustration. "I have no idea what you three are ranting about. How could I be covering up a murder I didn't even know about? Why would anyone have murdered Maddie's father anyway? What the fuck is going on?"

Logan finally let go of me to march toward Beckett, his massive frame looming over the other guy, who was half a foot shorter. "If one more lie comes out of that mouth—"

I leapt forward and snatched the back of Logan's shirt, yanking him to a halt. "Enough with the threats and the accusations. I want to know what the hell is going on too! Whatever it is you think you know, tell us." I couldn't decide whether it was remotely reasonable or if my other boyfriends had gone insane until I had some idea what had gotten them so riled up.

Slade's hand had slid down my arm to grasp my fingers when I'd lunged after Logan. "He owns that night club in town," he said tightly. "He was there at least one of the nights when we went dancing, before you ever talked to him. I bet he never told you that. He was stalking you."

"Preparing for your 'chance' meeting," Logan added, his voice dripping with derision.

Beckett raised his hands, his mouth tightening. "Yes, my *family* owns a club downtown. It's part of the family business. I swing by to check up on things periodically. I don't see how it's lying that I didn't tell you that when you never asked me about it. How was I supposed to realize you'd find it so suspicious? Do you need a full list of all my family's assets?"

"That would be a good start," Dexter piped up as if he hadn't realized it was a rhetorical question. I couldn't tell whether he was joking or serious.

My mind was reeling. It wasn't totally bizarre that Beckett might own the club and simply not mentioned it, but he definitely hadn't mentioned seeing me there. It *had* been just an accident that I'd bumped into him the one day outside the coffee shop… and the second time another day in the post office… hadn't it? Or had that been more than a welcome coincidence?

I caught his gaze. "Had you already seen me at the club before the first time we talked?"

Beckett looked back at me without a flicker of hesitation. "What does it matter? Would it really change anything if I had?"

He hadn't actually answered the question. A little chill quivered down my spine. "It might—if that means you went out of your way to make sure we'd end up talking as if it was a random meeting, when really you'd planned it all along."

Logan's lips had drawn back from his teeth in a silent growl. "He's got connections to the trucking company too. When we went to investigate it, we saw a truck with a shipment for his club, ordered in his name. We're supposed to believe it's just random chance that he's associated with a company that's got ties to all those other businesses in the trail we've followed—a company that probably also ships illegal merchandise?"

My stomach plummeted. Too many coincidences adding up tended to mean they weren't coincidental after all.

Beckett *had* turned up right after my car had gotten stolen—right after someone in town had realized I might have information to do with my dad.

I took a step back, tugging Logan with me. Beckett's eyes widened.

"Maddie," he said, "you can't really be buying into this bullshit. Clubs need to get shipments of alcohol. Someone's got to deliver them. There's nothing nefarious about it."

Slade snorted. "There is when you had so many other options and you just happened to pick the company that's mixed up in this case. And—" He cut himself off, his mouth setting in a grim line that wasn't like the joking, flirty guy I was used to at all. "We're not telling you everything we found out. You'll just use the information to make excuses and hurt even more people."

Beckett rubbed the bridge of his nose as if he had a headache. "I think I'm starting to get an inkling of what must have happened. Did someone you talked to today give you the impression that I was involved in whatever happened to Maddie's father? Whatever exactly happened, *they* were lying to you, probably to mess with this 'case' of yours. I didn't know anything about Maddie or her family until a month ago."

"You really expect us to believe that?" Logan said with a bark of dark laughter.

"There's an easy way to confirm it one way or the other," Beckett said. His usual air of confidence was coming back, his bewilderment smoothing away so easily.

Before, I'd admired his sense of calm. Now I couldn't help thinking it was incredibly strange that he could keep his cool in a situation like this. It made me wonder how many hostile people he'd had to face before, under what circumstances. This standoff wasn't anything like a standard business meeting.

Dexter cocked his head, his expression still tense. "What's that?"

"Tell me who spoke to you, where, and exactly what they said," Beckett replied. "I know a lot of people in this city. It shouldn't take long for me to determine who's behind the false accusation—and whoever that is, they're most likely the ones you should be yelling at. Why would they point you in the wrong direction if they weren't trying to protect themselves?"

"Right," Slade said skeptically. "And it's not at all that *you* want to point us in the wrong direction now."

Beckett ignored him and focused on me, his gaze

unwavering. "Maddie, you know I'd never hurt you. I swear I had no idea about this investigation or anything to do with your dad—and if anyone working for my family was involved, I'd know about it. Someone is trying to screw me over and using you to do it. Let me help you figure this out."

"We're not accepting 'help,'"—Logan made air quotes around the word, his voice dripping with hostile sarcasm—"from a person who has been in the middle of the situation all along without ever saying anything."

I opened my mouth and closed it again. I wanted to believe Beckett. He sounded so sure—but that was part of the reason I hesitated. He had an explanation for everything. He was barely even fazed by the guys accusing him of being tangled up in a murder.

He'd obviously hidden some small things from me. What if he'd hidden bigger things as well? The Vigil guys wouldn't be this worked up without plenty of reason, would they?

I grimaced, my throat tightening. "I think you should go," I said to Beckett. "I need some time to figure out what to think."

"Maddie, you can't really believe—"

I shook my head. "I don't know what to believe, Beckett. Please, just leave. I can't think while we're arguing like this."

He opened his mouth to speak again but closed it before any words escaped. With a stiff nod, he stepped back. "Can I call you?"

I shook my head. "I'd rather you didn't. I'll call *you* when I'm ready."

If I'm ever ready, I didn't bother saying. Or would the next call I made involving Beckett be to the police?

"Then I'll respect that request." Beckett's voice stayed even, but his hands were balled at his sides as he walked back to his car. I watched him get in and drive away, my spirits seeming to sink farther as he vanished from view.

Then I whirled toward the Vigil guys. "What exactly happened? Do you have more proof tying him to my dad's case than what you just said? Something we could bring to the cops?"

Logan scowled, which answered my last question all on its own. "No. Nothing concrete. But we talked to a guy who works for Beckett, who saw us scoping out the trucking company. He was scared to talk to us but made himself do it—he told us outright that Beckett's family is behind the murder of Evan Silver and that Beckett has been taking steps to cover it up. How would he know about any of that?"

He could if Beckett was right and someone who was really involved in the crimes was trying to frame Beckett. But why would anyone want to do that?

I swallowed a groan of frustration. "Do you think that guy would go to the police and tell them his story?"

Slade shook his head dejectedly. "He seemed panicky enough about telling us. I can't imagine him talking to the cops. If we could even find him again to ask him to. He wouldn't give us his name."

"He seemed like he was scared for his life," Dexter put in.

My stomach knotted. "What about leaving some kind of anonymous tip with the police so they'll investigate the same things we have, and we see what they turn up?"

Logan shook his head. "We can't leave a tip about a murder they don't have any record of happening, especially one that's twelve years cold. They'd think it was some crazy person and write it off." He squeezed my shoulder, his stance turning from threatening to protective in an instant. "But we'll figure it out. We've put a little fear into Beckett. Maybe he'll make a careless move that'll reveal more of his hand. We'll have to keep a close eye on the trucking company."

"And on Maddie," Dexter said quietly.

I knit my brow at him. "What are you talking about?"

Slade's smile came back for the first time, if muted. "Dex is trying to say that he's worried about you. We all are. When we saw you with that guy…" His fingers tightened around mine.

"You should come back to our apartment rather than staying in your dorm," Logan said in a definitive tone. "We can make sure you're safe."

"Safe?" I repeated. "You don't really think…"

My stepbrother's expression turned even more somber. "If Beckett has been covering up the murder, then he's behind your mom's accident and the fire in our office. Now that we've got him on the defensive, there's no telling what he might do next. If we could have gotten you away from him without revealing anything… but who knows what he was already planning…" He sighed. "He's dangerous. And next time, he might come after you."

CHAPTER
TWO

Beckett

"I need an idea of what they could have found here," I told the owner of Roadway Express Trucking, standing in the doorway to his office.

My jaw had been clenched tight since turning my back on Maddie and walking away, and I'd come straight here for information. If the other guys had come here in their amateur investigation and uncovered information that tied me to a murder, I needed to know how that had happened.

It *shouldn't* have happened, because I didn't know about any crimes involving Maddie's father, and the people under me wouldn't have been carrying out random hits.

The trucking company owner was scowling as he skimmed through the security camera footage that showed some of the main bay. "They claimed they were here as potential clients. Justin said it seemed like they were sniffing around for more than that, so he was careful about what he said, but you know the boys would never have shared anything it wasn't their business to either way."

"I certainly hope not," I said, firmly but calmly. "There'd be major consequences if it turned out someone under your employment was sabotaging my family's reputation."

The tensing of the man's stance told me he knew just how severe those consequences could be. He raised his chin. "I'm careful about who I hire, and I oversee them closely. There aren't any snitches or backstabbers around here."

He paused the footage and pointed to Maddie's three guys standing by one of the smaller trucks. "That's the only way they could have associated you with the company. That truck was being loaded with the latest shipment for your club. But you can see we were quick to make sure they couldn't examine the manifest or anything like that. Right afterward, the manager sent them off."

"No one talked to them except him?"

The owner shook his head. "And he said they didn't ask much other than basic business questions. None of them mentioned you or any concerns about the activities we're involved in."

I rubbed my forehead. I could see for myself that the workers in the bay had barely acknowledged the three guys besides some wary glances. No one had really talked to them in view of the camera other than to tell them to clear out.

Most of the employees weren't even aware of the shadier side of this company's operations. And making up a story about the murder of a man from twelve years ago in a town two hours from here would have been pretty bizarre.

"All right," I said, restraining a sigh. "Thank you for your help. Tell your people not to admit those three into the building again if they come around to badger you more."

The owner nodded with a swift jerk of his head. "I was already planning on that."

I stalked out of the office and glanced up and down the street as I headed to my car. Nothing about the neighborhood offered any clues either. Had the guys gotten suspicious simply because of a couple of random connections that as far as I could see had nothing to do with Maddie and her family at all? It didn't make any sense.

There were obviously pieces of the puzzle I was missing, and they hadn't wanted to tell me about those key factors. I supposed if they saw me as a murderer, that wasn't surprising, but it was pretty fucking frustrating all the same.

As I slid into the driver's seat, I pulled out my phone. If anything had changed in the day-to-day operations of the Storm's holdings, the woman Dad had turned to as a general manager for the past fifteen years should know about it.

Lana picked up on the second ring, her tone briskly efficient. "Beckett, what can I do for you today?"

"Hey, Lana," I said, willing the frustration out of my voice. "I've encountered a bit of a… situation involving our business, and I was hoping you might be able to shed some light on it. Are you aware of any unusual behavior from groups our people might have clashed with in the past or signs that another organization might be on the attack, even if it's only in subtle ways?"

She paused, with a few clicks on the other end as she must have glanced through whatever data she had available on her computer, double-checking. "No. If anything like that had come to my attention, I'd have notified you and your father right away, naturally."

"I know. But even if it was so small you didn't think it was worth worrying about yet—"

There was a rustle as she must have shaken her head. "I can't think of anything that would fit your question. Why are you asking? What's the specific concern?"

My jaw clenched even tighter, an ache running through my gums. I forced it to relax and closed my eyes for a second. The ache seemed to travel down into my chest.

I didn't want to explain the specific circumstances to her. It was too personal. She wouldn't understand what Maddie meant to me—and if she hadn't seen anything unusual at all, she definitely didn't know about someone framing my family for murder.

"I think it's better I handle this on my own for now," I said. "It may end up being a completely personal matter. I just wanted to confirm that nothing related had come up on your end." I paused. There was one person who could have carried out a murder and a cover-up without feeling the need to inform me. "My father hasn't given you any orders recently that you haven't kept me in the loop on, has he?"

"I always make sure to coordinate between the two of you," she said, which was a diplomatic answer. I suspected she hadn't heard anything from Dad in a week if not longer. We both knew that I handled almost all of the Storm's operations these days.

"I know you do. Again, just wanted to confirm. I appreciate you humoring me."

"Any time, Beckett. And if something does come to my attention that seems at all concerning, I'll notify you at once."

The drive home didn't do anything to soothe my nerves, no matter how many slow, steady breaths I made myself take. In the back of my head, I kept seeing Logan yanking Maddie away from me. The three guys glaring at me like *I'd* ripped her father from her life. Maddie's expression shifting as she realized that I hadn't been completely above board with her on the subject of my business dealings—and how I'd first noticed her.

I couldn't let my emotions cloud my judgment. I

needed to consider every possibility until I'd gotten answers. Whoever had gotten to the guys had it in for my family, and stopping them before they did more damage of any kind had to be my first priority.

There was a small chance that Dad had done something in the past that I wasn't aware of and that it was so long ago Lana wouldn't have thought of the incident. After all, I'd have been only eleven when Maddie's father had died. Faking illnesses wasn't a technique I'd ever heard of our people using, but I couldn't assume I knew everything.

I passed through the electric gate and parked in the five-car garage. Our big suburban house on the outskirts of the city was where I'd spent the majority of my life when we weren't on the move handling business transactions and overseeing activities elsewhere. It was home, but it often didn't feel like one these days. Because the moment I walked through the door into the expansive front hall, I sensed the gloom that had fallen over the place.

That, and the faint voices from a distant TV. I followed them to the family room and found Dad sitting back in his recliner, the remote on the arm next to his hand. Evening was falling outside, the sunlight dwindling, but he hadn't bothered to turn on the lights. The TV's glow cut starkly into the room. His gaze flicked to me and then back to the screen without so much as a hello, his expression slack.

I studied him for a moment, trying to imagine this shell of a man launching an attack on Maddie and her other boyfriends. It was hard to picture him summoning enough conviction to bother. Lately, he'd only given the most cursory attention to our basic dealings. Why would he go out of his way to stir up more trouble over a long-cold murder?

But I couldn't ignore the possibility completely, not when everything about this scenario seemed ridiculous.

"Hey, Dad," I said. "Any thoughts on dinner?"

His gaze returned to me, but I felt like he wasn't totally seeing me. He waved his hand dismissively. "I'm sure whatever Emilio whips up will be fine."

Fair enough. I inhaled deeply, steadying myself. "True. I'm looking forward to it. By the way, a name came up today as someone who might have interfered with our operations at some point—Evan Silver? Does that ring any bells?"

Dad frowned, but he looked more annoyed that I was making him think than concerned about a possible business problem. "I can't think of anyone by that name. Did he work with one of the other families?"

The Devil's Dozen families, he meant. I shook my head. "Not as far as I know. He was a doctor. A researcher at Southwestern Regional Memorial Hospital." I'd looked up the one hospital in the area of Maddie's hometown, based on what she'd told me before about her father's work.

The air of confusion lingered around my dad. I could tell he had no idea what I was talking about, which relieved me even as his lack of investment niggled at me.

"None of that sounds at all familiar," he said definitively. "If you find out he damaged our holdings in some way, I'm sure you know how to deal with that." His attention slid back to the TV.

"I do. No need to worry about it." Not that he looked like he was particularly worried anyway.

I stepped out of the room and hesitated in the hallway. The ache in my chest tightened.

Years ago, I'd have been able to turn to Dad for guidance. I could have laid the situation out, and he'd have considered it from every angle alongside me, suggesting strategies and avenues of inquiry. But even if I tried to tell him I needed help, he wouldn't be able to offer much these days. He just didn't care enough. He'd probably tell me I should be proving myself, not leaning on him.

All because of the choices I'd made trying to prove myself and protect the family before, which had shattered his faith in both me and himself in the process.

I swallowed hard and headed upstairs, but my own worries chased at my heels. Yes, someone clearly had it in for me and the Storm, but I'd handled vengeful assholes before. I wasn't afraid of that.

I *was* afraid for Maddie. It didn't matter what kind of hotshots her other guys believed they were. They couldn't be prepared to tangle with the sorts of criminals who ran in my family's circle, the few who were even aware of our level of society. Whoever *was* behind the cover up and the murder was obviously dangerous. The threat the guys had decided I represented was still out there, unknown, maybe already planning another attack.

My hands closed into fists at my sides. I couldn't stand back and watch someone hurt her. I needed to know what they'd uncovered so I could deal with it *my* way.

But the guys were never going to be on board with that, not now. Our confrontation this afternoon had made that painfully clear. They'd never really trusted me in the first place, and whatever they'd heard had only confirmed their suspicions.

I had to get through to Maddie. I had to make her understand why I'd told the lies I had and that they had nothing to do with the threats she was facing now. That I could protect her from those threats. I didn't want to lose another person because they didn't understand why I'd done the things I'd done or how much they mattered to me.

But what the hell could I say to her that would convince her while the three of them had her ear and I'd been pushed aside?

I paced in my bedroom for several minutes before sitting down on the edge of the bed and getting out my phone again. If I couldn't talk to my dad, there were other people who'd been a guiding force for me after he'd pulled away. Everyone in Paradise Bend had my back, but Rowan had taken me under his wing more than anyone from the start.

I hit his name in my contacts and tipped backward on the bed.

The phone had almost gone to voicemail when Rowan picked up, his familiar easygoing tenor sounding a little harried. "Beckett?"

A childish voice was chattering in the background on a rant about jellybeans. The corners of my mouth twitched upward. "Sorry if I'm interrupting something. Busy with the kids?"

He chuckled. "Always." He paused and muttered something off the line, and a lower rumble of a voice I recognized as Kaige's carried from farther away. The little girl squealed with laughter as he must have swooped in.

Rowan came back, a little more relaxed now. "The baby went down a few minutes ago, but Josey'll do anything to delay bedtime. That's four-year-olds for you. What's up?"

I could tell he could actually talk now. "I just wondered how you're all doing."

Rowan hummed, probably able to tell it was more than that but playing along while I worked up to my real question. "About as well as we can with the new baby keeping us up at all hours. At least we've got plenty of us to spread the sleeplessness around! Mercy's already back on the job, laying down the law with her people and telling off anyone who thinks a mom can't keep them in line."

I snorted. "They'll regret that mistake fast." Mercy

was just about the toughest person I knew, man or woman.

"Oh, believe me, they do."

He paused, and I could feel him leaving an opening for me to get to the real point. I stared up at the ceiling for a moment before saying, "How do you handle it when she's in danger? Like before, when Xavier was terrorizing her, and all the other stuff that goes on around her... How do you keep your cool and figure out the best way to help her rather than going batshit trying to protect her?"

Rowan's voice softened. "Sounds like someone speaking from new experience. Congrats if you've found a woman who means enough to you that you'd go batshit for her."

I glowered at the ceiling. "That doesn't really help."

He gave a light laugh. "I know. I guess..." His tone turned more serious. "I just decided I'd do whatever it took to make sure she got through okay. Even if *I* got hurt instead. Even if I put my whole life on the line. No holds barred. I love her, and I wouldn't feel right standing back if there was anything at all I could do. Knowing I'm that committed, that I'll take whatever action I need to, makes it easier for me to simmer down long enough to figure out what the best action would be. If that makes sense?"

The sentiments he'd expressed about how far he'd go rang completely true. "Yeah," I said. "It does."

"So you do have someone like that now?"

I thought of Maddie—of her smile, of the passion

that came over her face when she talked about her future plans, of the mix of affection and determination in her kiss. My fingers tightened around the phone.

"Yeah. And I would do anything for her, so you're right. I've just got to figure out what the right thing is, the thing that'll protect her the most."

CHAPTER
THREE

Madelyn

I used my chopsticks to pick at the small carton of rice that had been drowned in the sweet and sour chicken from a local Chinese restaurant. The Vigil guys were all digging into their own cartons around their apartment's living room, though Dexter had opted to use a fork, looking as if he wasn't totally pleased that he hadn't had time to cook while we tried to work out what Beckett's full connection to their investigation might be.

He popped a mouthful of lo mein into his mouth while peering intently at the shipping records with the trucking company logo that Slade had grabbed several days ago. The records had been in an envelope tacked to the door of a shell corporation we'd tied to two other businesses it was clear Dad had been looking into, but we hadn't figured out how the trucking company fit in.

From Dexter's expression, he wasn't getting any closer. He flipped to the second page and sighed. "There's definitely no way I can break the code on this without the key. And no way to figure out what that key is."

"I bet Beckett knows," Logan muttered darkly as he scanned through our surveillance camera footage on his laptop.

"We still haven't found any evidence that proves his family has anything to do with my dad's death," I reminded him. "Nothing connecting him to the warehouse Dad had the address to or the seafood market that was receiving deliveries from them—that had the logo he mentioned when he was sick. You're trying your best to pin this on him, and it's still not sticking."

Logan looked up to briefly glower at me. "He's a crook. He lied to us, and one of his employees was so wracked with guilt the guy spilled the beans. Don't defend him."

I guessed I should be glad Logan didn't say anything harsher considering how close I'd gotten to our supposed enemy. But I still couldn't shake the sense that nothing about this felt totally right.

There was definitely more going on with Beckett than I'd realized, but he'd never asked me anything about my dad other than a couple of typical questions when I'd brought up his death. I hadn't gotten the slightest sense that he was checking whether I knew about the murder or had evidence he might need to destroy.

"What about your tour of the spa?" Slade asked, waving his chopsticks at me. "We've barely had time to go over that. Maybe something you saw there will connect the dots."

I tipped my head back, letting my vision go vague as I reached into my memories. I'd stopped by a spa that was another business under the same shell corporation as the warehouse and the seafood market earlier today, hoping to get a better idea of what the overall organization was involved with.

"I did see some sketchy stuff," I said. "It looked like they might be selling drugs to some of their clientele, pretending it's a special service. I caught a hand-off of the drugs on video—that might work as evidence. But it's got nothing to do with Beckett."

When he'd picked me up, he hadn't seemed at all concerned that I might have learned something incriminating about him there. Although he had acted pretty protective in general… maybe like he had some reason to believe the place might be dangerous beyond my urgent appeal for help.

But if he'd been worried about crimes he was involved in being exposed, I'd have expected a much different reaction. He'd only seemed concerned about my well-being.

How could that guy have been responsible for causing my mom's car accident? How could he have set fire to the Vigil office knowing I might be in there?

A different part of the memory clicked in my head. "I did see the woman who was at the bar the day I snuck in and got my dad's trinket box back. The one who was part of the gang running the place." The one who'd nearly shot Logan when the guys had charged in to help me escape.

Slade perked up. "Then there is a common thread between all of them."

"All of the places where we've found evidence related to my dad," I said. "Those documents we can't even read are the only things that tie Beckett to any of the rest, and even that evidence is shaky. He was getting a delivery from the trucking company. He might not be any more involved in the business than that."

Logan grunted abruptly. I thought he was making a wordless objection to my point until I glanced over and saw his attention was completely focused on his laptop screen.

"The camera's down," he said.

All of us immediately gathered around the armchair where he was sitting. The window open on the screen was totally blank other than the small words *NO SIGNAL* in the middle.

"Which one's that?" Slade asked.

Logan opened a different window, which showed the same thing. "This is at the office building where the shell corporation was located. Both of the feeds are down—the one in the hall outside and the one by the front entrance. That's got to mean someone found them and purposefully disabled them, not that one got bumped by accident or something."

Dexter considered the screen as avidly as he had the trucking company documents. "When did they cut out? Do you think Beckett went looking after we confronted him?"

"Let me see…" Logan skimmed back through the recorded footage and found the last section where there was actual video showing. The time and date stamp in the bottom corner was just after eight last night. One feed went black, and then the other followed a minute later. It definitely looked like someone had gone and found both.

"The cameras at the seafood market are still running," Logan said. "No one's discovered those yet."

A sinking feeling pulled at my stomach. "This *really* doesn't make sense. They were disabled before you accused Beckett. And if he's at the center of this conspiracy and someone found those cameras pointed at a key site last night, wouldn't they have reported it to him? Shouldn't he have realized we were on to him?"

Slade cocked his head. "Maybe he did. He must have already known we were poking around, or he wouldn't have gone after your mom or our office to try to threaten us into backing off."

I threw my hands in the air. "But he seemed totally confused when you guys confronted him this afternoon. Like he had no idea what you were talking about."

"Maybe he's just a good actor," Logan muttered.

"Then wouldn't he have come up with a better story? He wasn't prepared at all for the accusations you threw at him or the questions I asked. We didn't shove any real proof at him. It shouldn't have been hard for him to come up with a fake explanation that would make it all seem reasonable if he'd known in advance that the subject might come up."

Logan snapped his computer shut, his expression stormy. "Or he just wanted you to think that. You can't let your emotions get tangled up in this, Maddie."

I folded my arms over my chest. "Like your emotions aren't? I'm sure you've been champing at the bit for an excuse to hate Beckett from the first second I mentioned he existed."

He scowled at me, but he didn't deny it.

Dexter cleared his throat and rested a tentative hand on my shoulder—just for a second, but his touch was rare enough to send a heated shiver through me before he withdrew it.

"The only solid connection we do have between Beckett and Maddie's dad is the employee who told us about it," he said. "We're not getting anywhere with the records we have here. We should see what else we can find out about that guy. Maybe if we track him down, we can convince him to go to the police with what he knows or hand some real evidence over to us after all."

Okay, that was a plan I could at least partly get behind. I nodded, shooting Dexter a grateful smile. "How would we do that?"

Slade tapped his lips. "The only place we saw him was by the trucking company."

Logan sprang out of his chair, aggressive energy radiating off his brawny frame. "Let's head back there then, and see if there's anything we can make use of in the area."

We tramped down to the parking lot and piled into Logan's car, Slade sliding into the backseat next to me. He reached across the seat to twine his fingers with mine, but tension hummed through the air. All of us were on edge as we waited to find out if this course of action would finally get us somewhere.

Logan drove swiftly along the darkened roads. "It's just up here," he said as we approached the trucking company. He leaned forward to squint at the storefronts nearby, lit up by the yellowed glow of the streetlamps.

"There," Dexter said, pointing at something beyond the windshield. "That convenience store has a security cam out front at an angle that probably caught the other side of the street."

"Perfect." Logan pulled over to the sidewalk just down the street. "Let's check it out."

I'd been around the Vigil guys enough that I didn't bother to question *how* we were going to manage that. Their methods weren't always what you could call legit. Or legal. But they did get the job done, and right now, we needed answers.

Dexter had already pulled out his lock picks before we'd made it around the side of the convenience store to its back door. He made quick work of the lock and nudged the door open. The interior of the store was dark and silent, no one around this late at night.

"No other security system," Dexter murmured. "They probably can't afford anything much."

"Makes it easier for us." Slade slunk down the hall and paused at a room just before the larger area up ahead where I could see shelves lined with merchandise. "I think this is the manager's office. There's a computer."

Logan flexed his hands. "My turn to do the breaking and entering."

He stepped ahead of Slade into the small office room and dropped into the chair at the metal desk. As his fingers whipped across the keyboard, sending the monitor flickering to life, the rest of us gathered behind him.

I couldn't tell what he was doing exactly, but after a couple of minutes of clicking and tapping, the password request window vanished, and the regular desktop full of icons appeared before us. Logan grinned tightly and sent the cursor veering across the screen. "Ah ha. Looks like the footage is stored here. Usually these kind of systems are set up to delete after no less than twenty-four hours, so this morning's footage should definitely still be there."

He opened up the folder and skimmed through the file names, which seemed to be labeled by the day and hour. Then he clicked one open. It showed a view of the sidewalk outside the shop—and the road and the trucking company building on the other side just ahead, as Dexter had predicted.

Slade let out an approving whistle and gave his friend a thumbs up. "Now we're talking."

Logan played the footage at three times the normal speed, racing through various people coming and going from the trucking company door and its bay off to the side. I guessed none of the guys spotted the man who'd approached them, because none of them said a word. Then Logan clicked the mouse to bring the video feed back to regular playback, just as I saw the three guys currently around me walking up to the building.

They stepped in through the front door, and Slade let out an urgent sound next to me. He pointed at the screen.

The second after the Vigil guys had entered the building, a gangly man with slicked-back hair had strode into view from the same direction they'd arrived from. He walked briskly but confidently toward the trucking company.

Dexter knit his brow. "That's him, but he doesn't look nervous at all. The opposite, really. He seemed so anxious when he approached us."

Slade frowned. "Where's he going now?"

The man had veered down the alley next to the trucking company instead of continuing on to the door. He stopped there, standing where he was only just visible in the shadows near the mouth of the alley, braced as if waiting for something.

"It looks like he followed you there and then hung out until you left," I said. "I thought you said it seemed like he only noticed you after you showed up?"

"Maybe he'd spotted us somewhere we were investigating earlier and…" Logan paused, clearly not sure how to explain how the man would have tracked him down again. "Or he could have just seen us from farther down the street when we pulled up."

I guessed that was possible.

The man stayed in place until the Vigil guys emerged several minutes later. They continued down the street, clustered close together in conversation. As they passed out of view of the camera, the man in the alley edged closer, clearly having noticed their presence. He waited for several beats and then slipped out onto the sidewalk.

As he headed after the guys, his posture slumped, his head ducking and his shoulders hunching. His head jerked with nervous twitches as he scanned the street. Then he vanished from the frame too.

Logan stopped the playback, staring grimly at the screen. I knew he had to have noticed how strange this was too.

"It's like he planned out how he'd talk to you," I said. "He only acted nervous when he knew you were about to see him. It *was* an act."

"Or maybe he started out confident and then got freaked out as the possible consequences of blabbing on his boss sank in?" Slade said, but he couldn't put a lot of conviction into the suggestion.

I hugged myself. "I don't know what's going on here, but I don't like it at all. Too much doesn't add up."

"It doesn't add up because we don't have all the

pieces yet," Logan said stubbornly, but he was obviously just as uncertain as the rest of us.

I didn't know if he was letting himself think this far yet, but I couldn't help it. What if Beckett's confusion had been completely real? What if he really had been set up?

What if we were focusing all this energy on blaming him when the real villain was still lurking behind the scenes, ready to strike again?

CHAPTER
FOUR

Slade

groaned as I came into consciousness, stretching my legs out to relieve the stiffness in my back. The couch was comfortable to lounge on while watching TV, but not the greatest for a full night's sleep. My joints cracked as I sat upright with a brief yawn. The scent of last night's Chinese food still hung in the air, provoking a gurgle in my stomach.

Logan was just stuffing a couple of textbooks into his bag near the front door. He glanced over at me when I moved and offered an apologetic grimace, keeping his voice low. "I hope I didn't wake you up."

I shook my head. "Happened all on its own."

He slung his backpack over his shoulder with a huff of frustration. "Have to get to class. It seems stupid even *having* classes while all this shit is going down."

"At least they're teaching you skills that'll make you an even better hacker," I said with a half-hearted grin. "Whether they meant to do that or not."

"One can only hope."

"We won't do too much work without you. Gotta make sure you're still carrying your weight."

Logan snorted and gave me the middle finger as he walked out of the apartment. As the deadbolt clicked into place behind him, I grabbed my prosthetic from where I'd left it on the armchair, fixed it onto my stump, and ambled over to my bedroom.

The hinges squeaked faintly when I eased the door slightly open. Maddie didn't stir from where she'd sprawled amid my bedsheets. I sent up a silent offering of gratitude that I'd washed them recently.

When we'd gotten back from our investigations last night, we'd all been too wiped to do anything other than crash. Logan had tried to nobly offer *his* bed to Maddie while he took the couch, but I'd had to point out that he was way too tall to get any sleep that way. He'd barely fit on the thing. So he'd grudgingly allowed me to make the gesture and take the minor discomfort.

Did I regret it? Not at all.

Did the crick in my neck have me wincing as I turned my head? Yes, absolutely.

But seeing the way she lay there so peacefully made every bit of discomfort worth it. I'd give up a hundred restful nights to see her sleep like this. She'd been under so much pressure over the past few weeks—first because of the situation with Logan and her stolen car, and then with her dad's murder.

I wished I could do more to help her through this mess, but offering my bed seemed to be the most I could manage. Aside from jokes and fun, I wasn't much good at anything else. Showing off my language skills wasn't going to fix anything. Even if we found the people responsible for this murder, it wouldn't be because of me. Dexter and Logan were the brains and strategists behind this investigation.

I was just… here. Providing moral support and an extra set of eyes and hands—that was about it.

Dexter emerged from his bedroom on the other side of the living room, his dark curls even more rumpled than usual and the boxers and tee he'd worn to sleep in a similar state. He padded across the floor to join me and peeked past me at our sleeping girlfriend.

"She was really tired, huh?" he murmured.

"We went through a lot yesterday."

"No kidding." A fond smile touched his lips, a glow of affection lighting in his eyes that I didn't think I'd ever seen from my typically anti-social friend before. "But she's taking it all in and keeping up with the rest of us, even though she's not used to situations like this. She really is something."

"I've never met a woman like her," I agreed.

Dexter paused and swiped his hand across his mouth with a hint of his usual awkwardness. His voice dipped even quieter. "I don't know if I'm going to be enough for her."

My head jerked around so I could stare at him. "What are you talking about?"

He shrugged. "I just—obviously she's got you and Logan too. It's not like I'm in this alone. But I want her to be happy that she's with me too. I don't have any real experience with relationships—romance, sex, any of it. I have no idea what I'm doing, not like the two of you. And... it's not exactly a secret that I'm what most people would call weird."

I aimed a playful punch at his shoulder, not quite making contact since he wasn't much of one for physical touch. "Your weirdness is your best quality. You'll be good for her in totally different ways from the two of us. Maybe she'll even decide she likes you best."

Dexter's expression remained doubtful. Looking from him to our dozing woman, inspiration sparked in my head. A small smile curled my lips. Maybe I couldn't offer a whole lot, but I could certainly deliver more of the stuff I was good at.

"Hey," I said, tipping my head toward Dexter. "You know, Logan and I were able to, ah, work well together when it came to giving her a good time. I don't see any reason you and I couldn't do the same. Why don't we start off this morning by giving her something fantastic to remember amid all the awfulness that's been going on?"

Dexter's gaze flicked to me, desire flaring in his eyes

alongside the affection I'd seen earlier. "You think she'd like that?"

"Oh, I bet we could make sure she likes it an awful lot. And I could give you some tips from my vast expertise." I grinned at him. "Totally up to you if you're comfortable with it."

He wet his lips, looking at Maddie again. "Yeah," he said softly. "That could be good. Just to make sure I'm not missing anything. And so she gets as much out of it as possible."

From the way he'd been observing her since she'd joined our investigations, I didn't think it was likely there was much he hadn't figured out or couldn't if the right moment arose. He probably knew more about Maddie's little quirks than I did. But by collaborating, we could give her more than either of us could on our own. And she deserved every bit of pleasure she could get while we had a chance to bestow it on her.

As if she'd sensed our discussion, Maddie rolled over on the bed. She rubbed her eyes and spotted us in the doorway.

"Good morning?" she mumbled questioningly, squinting at us. "Did I sleep in?"

"Not too much." I stepped into the room. "How are you feeling?"

"Other than completely confused by this mystery we can't seem to unravel, pretty good." She raised her eyebrows at me and Dexter following behind me. "So, you were just watching me sleep? Some people would consider that strange."

"Or romantic. What do you think, Dex?"

"It was a little strange," he said, and I narrowed my eyes at him.

Maddie cracked a laugh and sat up in bed, allowing the sheets to fall to her waist. "I can always count on Dexter to have my back."

She'd slept in the tank top she'd had on under her sweater but taken off her bra, her nipples lightly pebbled against the thin fabric. My dick twitched to attention at the sight.

"Hmph," I said in mock-annoyance, and sat down on the bed to grab one of her feet. "But I have your foot."

I dug my thumbs into the arch in a firm massage, and Maddie relaxed back on her hands, flexing her ankle. "Feel free to keep having it if that's what you're going to do with it. I hope the couch wasn't too uncomfortable."

"It was fine," I said, and teased my thumb over her toes. "Of course, I'd have enjoyed sharing this bed with you even more, but I don't think we'd have gotten much sleep that way."

Amusement warmed Maddie's expression. "Is that so?"

"Oh, definitely. So I made that immense sacrifice for the sake of our health. But of course now that we *have* gotten some sleep…"

I let my hands slide over her ankle to her calf. She'd taken off her jeans to sleep, and my fingers kneaded silky skin. She mustn't have anything on beneath the sheet other than her panties. My cock got even harder just picturing her.

Maddie hummed happily. "I'm so curious to see what you have in mind." Her eyelids had lowered, but she lifted them again to glance at Dexter, who was still standing by the corner of the bed, his hands at his sides. "And did you have big plans too?"

Her tone immediately gentled when she spoke to him, and a rush of affection swept through me. It was obvious she understood how uncertain he was about this kind of intimacy. She didn't want to force anything on him too quickly.

She got him in a way so many other women hadn't —she appreciated what made him such an amazing guy, weird or not. How could *I* not love that about her?

Dexter's tongue flicked over his lips again, his gaze glued to her. "Absolutely. If you'd like both of us."

A brilliant smile stretched across her face. "Both sounds pretty amazing. Come here?"

It was definitely a question, not a demand, but Dexter moved as if pulled toward her. He knelt on the bed, his eyes never leaving her face. I half expected him to freeze up, for me or Maddie to have to encourage him onward, but he had more confidence than he'd given himself credit for. He raised his hand to stroke her cheek and then lowered his head to claim her mouth.

His kiss gave Maddie all the encouragement she must have needed to wind her arm around the back of his neck. As she kissed him back, I tugged the sheet off her legs and bent down to press my mouth to her shin.

My hands traveled farther, over her knee and partway up her thigh, massaging the whole way. Maddie let out her first small groan of pleasure against Dexter's lips. He made a strained sound of his own and kissed her harder.

Oh, it looked like my friend was a fast learner, all right.

He moved his mouth from her lips to her jaw and then down her neck as Maddie tipped her head back to give him better access. A sly smirk crossed my face.

"Use your teeth too," I suggested. "Just a little nip here and there. She likes that." As I well knew from the fun I'd had with her before.

Dexter must have taken my advice, because Maddie's next breath came out stuttered. "That's playing dirty."

I chuckled. "That's *exactly* what it is. But you'll reap all the benefits."

I slid my hands even higher, caressing the skin just below the apex of her thighs. Maddie squirmed at my touch, and I thought I could see a patch of dampness already forming on her peach-pink panties. My mouth watered at the thought of tasting her there like I had before. But I didn't want to take over the encounter too much, not while Dexter was still getting used to the idea of us sharing her.

Instead, I simply grazed the tips of my fingers over her pussy through the fabric. Maddie whimpered and dug her fingers into Dexter's curls. He didn't object when she yanked his mouth back to hers.

I fondled her lightly through her panties as their kisses turned more passionate. Dexter pulled away, but with no sign of being overwhelmed. He was keeping up better than I'd expected after his earlier doubts.

He worked both his hands under her tank top across her toned stomach and tugged the fabric up. Maddie raised her arms and let him peel the shirt off of her. Both he and I paused, taking in the expanse of pale skin he'd bared. Her breasts bounced slightly as she adjusted her position next to him, her rosy nipples perked.

Dexter cupped his hand around one breast and swiveled his thumb over the nipple to draw it to a stiffer peak. Maddie let out an eager murmur, a flush spreading up her neck and across her cheeks.

I wanted to be up there with her too, sucking those little noises into my mouth with a kiss, tasting those soft mounds, but somehow it was even more electrifying to watch Dexter work her over.

"Use your mouth too," I said raggedly. He could pleasure her on my behalf too.

When he dropped his head to suck the peak of her other breast between his lips, I resumed my delicate caresses between Maddie's legs. As her grip on Dexter's hair tightened, her eyes rolled upward with a moan. I couldn't help grinning even while my erection strained against my boxers.

God, I wanted her. She was absolutely fucking perfect.

"Ease back a bit," I murmured to Dexter, stroking a

little more firmly. Maddie's hips lifted to meet my touch. "Blow on her nipple and then lick it."

He followed my instructions, and Maddie shivered with bliss. The sight had me aching twice as hard as before. I couldn't stop myself from delving my other hand into my boxers, sliding them down my hips so I could grip my rigid cock.

"Good," I muttered, pumping myself hard while I watched.

Dexter nipped and licked and ghosted his breath over one breast and then the other, and Maddie writhed between us with those lovely sounds of pleasure. Then her gaze caught mine. Her eyes dipped lower to how I was occupying my other hand, and a glint of delight lit in them.

She tugged Dexter's head up to capture his mouth with one more kiss. Then she eased onto all fours, turning toward me as my fingers fell away from her panties.

"We should all be having fun," she said, running her tongue across her bottom lip.

"Oh, I am, Piccolina."

"But you could have even more."

She lowered her head to my lap and took the head of my cock into her mouth without hesitation. Fuck me. Her tongue swirled around my shaft, and a jolt of pure bliss shot through my dick, radiating through the rest of my body.

"Hell, yes, you bet I can," I rasped, but I couldn't let our woman stay unattended. "Dex, get those panties off her. Stroke her pussy until she's even wetter."

Dexter crawled closer and dipped his fingers between her legs from behind. Maddie gasped around my cock. She sucked me harder, and a groan reverberated from my chest.

I wasn't going to last very long like this.

But Maddie wasn't above a little teasing herself. She swiveled her tongue around me once more and then raised herself up to turn toward Dexter again. He didn't show a hint of resistance as she nudged his chest, pushing him down on his back so she could climb atop him. She rocked on his lap, her pussy brushing against the bulge of his erection behind his boxers. Dexter let out a guttural sound and arched to meet her.

Maddie grasped the waistband of his boxers and dragged them down before glancing around. "Condom?" she asked breathlessly.

I practically lunged for the bedside table where I kept my stash. I tore open the foil with my teeth before passing the packet to her.

Maddie flashed me a smile of lustful thanks before rolling the condom down Dexter's length. His chest heaved with anticipation, his eyes almost feverishly bright.

He didn't wait for her to initiate the final step. He grasped her hips and positioned her over him. They groaned together as she sank down and he bucked up, penetrating those slick folds in one go.

Heat flooded my body, and a need I couldn't deny

gripped my chest. I scooted across the mattress toward the pillows and tangled my fingers in the hair at the back of Maddie's head.

She glanced down at my straining erection and smiled dreamily. At my pull, she eased down while she kept rocking over Dexter and took me into her mouth again.

The choked sound that escaped me at the press of her lips was totally primal. I didn't hold myself back, tightening my grip on her hair and swaying my hips to fuck her mouth. Maddie took me down with eager swipes of her tongue and squeezes of her lips, still bucking with Dexter at the same time.

She sucked hard and flicked the flat of her tongue against the underside of my cock at the same time, and I came so fast I didn't have time to even grunt a warning. Pleasure raced through me, and I exploded in her mouth.

Maddie didn't so much as wince, swallowing down my cum as if it was the best drink she'd ever tasted. The pleasure lingered on as she slid her lips off of me.

Dexter reached up to fondle both of her breasts. Maddie sighed and rocked faster, their bodies smacking together as they chased their own release. I pinched her ass, gazing up at her passion-filled face.

"Let it all out, Piccolina. I want to hear it all. Every goddamned sound."

She obliged, opening her mouth to emit a deeper moan. "Fuck," Dexter muttered, his hips jerking faster. Every whimper and gasp that spilled from our woman's lips set me on fire all over again until her muscles clenched with her release.

Maddie tipped her head back, a shudder running through her torso. Dexter groaned and rammed into her even harder, his breath shattering when he followed.

They rocked to a stop, and Maddie sank down to sprawl between us. I nestled close to her, slipping my arm around her waist. Dexter rolled onto his side with a content expression and rested a careful hand on her hip.

"That's what you sound like when you're allowed to make noises," I mused, the thought of it bringing a grin to my face. "We need a replay."

Maddie giggled breathlessly. "Right now?"

"I need a few minutes if we're going to do anything like this again," Dexter admitted.

Maddie and I both laughed, and I nodded. "Me too, Dex. Maybe we'll wait for another day."

We all lay there and caught our breaths, but I couldn't tear my gaze from Maddie. Joy brightened her face. We were all sated and pleased with ourselves—and fully pleasured.

But as we relaxed in silence together, her eyes started to cloud with worries again. I could see the strain of them creeping across her expression.

No matter how hard I tried to make her happy, I hadn't gotten rid of the source of her stress. And I had no idea how I could.

CHAPTER
FIVE

Madelyn

As I stepped out of my last class of the afternoon, I let out my breath in a sigh and rolled my shoulders. The genetics seminar went over a lot of material I found fascinating, but it was getting harder to absorb all the information when my head felt so full of theories and possible evidence related to Dad's murder and Beckett's potential role in it.

I meandered a short distance down the hallway and resigned myself to plopping down on a bench by the wall, pulling out my phone to occupy myself. The Vigil guys all had classes during this time period that ended later than mine. Logan's had the closest timeframe, and he'd insisted that I should wait in the building by the lecture hall for the twenty minutes it'd take for his class to let out and him to hustle across the campus.

It seemed a little ridiculous that I'd need protection just to walk anywhere on campus, but Slade and Dexter had agreed with Logan. I hadn't felt like getting into a big argument with all of them. It wasn't as if I had anything urgent to do right this minute anyway, so I might as well humor them.

I scrolled through a couple of social media feeds, and then a text from Keeley popped up. My roommate sounded typically energetic even in text form.

Hey Maddie! You should swing by our room as soon as you can. The RA dropped off something for you—it looks pretty cool!

I knit my brow as I re-read the message. What would the RA have brought for me? I'd barely talked with the senior who oversaw our floor. But it could be that a package from home had come in and been misdirected, and she'd needed to bring it to me by hand. That would be just like Mom, only out of the hospital for a few days and sending something to cheer *me* up.

Hesitating, I glanced around the hallway. It looked the same as always, the students for the next class already filing into the seminar room, a few more lingering around chatting with each other. My dorm building was just a couple of minutes away, and Logan wasn't due for another fifteen. Why the hell shouldn't I quickly pop over and find out what "cool" thing I'd gotten?

Sure, I'll be right over, I texted back. *Thanks for letting me know!*

I set a brisk pace along the campus paths, not stopping to enjoy the warmth of the spring day. I'd prefer to get back to my waiting spot before Logan showed up so I could avoid whatever lecture he'd give me. In no time at all, I was climbing up the stairs in the dorm building and pushing into the hall.

I already had my keycard in hand when I reached the door to our room. I swiped it and headed inside, expecting to see Keeley waiting eagerly for me to discover my surprise.

She wasn't there. I stalled a couple of steps into the room, frowning as I took in our beds with their rumpled covers, my neat desk and hers with its chaos of binders and make-up, and the thin rug on the floor. I didn't see anything inside that hadn't been here the last time I'd been in the room either—no special deliveries. What the heck was going on?

My surprise had just given way to a jolt of apprehension when footsteps thudded behind me. I spun around just as Beckett strode into the room.

My pulse stuttered. A startled yelp burst from my throat, lost to the hall in the thump as Beckett shut the door behind him. I backed up to my desk and gripped my chair, wondering if I should scream for help.

Before I'd made a decision, Beckett raised his hands in a gesture of surrender. His mouth twisted at a pained angle, and he stayed at the opposite end of the room, giving me as much space as he could. His dark gray eyes pierced into mine. "I'm not going to hurt you. I'd *never* hurt you. I just want you to hear my side of the story—properly, without the other guys interrupting with accusations every few seconds."

My shoulders came down a tad, but I remained braced for a fight. "How am I supposed to trust you when you snuck up on me like this? How did you even get in here—what happened to Keeley?"

"I didn't hurt her either," Beckett said, slowly and calmly. "All I did was tell her I wanted to surprise you by showing up unexpectedly and ask her to send you a text to get you to come over. She was more than happy to support my romantic gesture." His voice turned a bit wry with the last few words, but he kept his hands in their submissive position.

Damn it. Keeley would have recognized Beckett from the photo I'd shown her of him—which she'd highly approved of—and it'd never occurred to me to tell her that I'd discovered he might be dangerous. I hadn't even seen her since I'd found that out myself.

"I would never hurt anyone you care about, and that includes your family," Beckett went on into my silence. "I swear to you that I had no idea your dad was murdered until yesterday. And I've never lied to you about how I feel about you. I just... wasn't completely upfront about everything *my* family is involved in, as far as our business goes. Will you please hear me out?"

My stomach churned as I sorted through my emotions. He'd scared me by making this impromptu visit—but only because of the fears the Vigil guys had planted in my head. Two days ago, his arrival would have been a pleasant surprise. Until yesterday, I'd never seen any reason to think Beckett had malicious intentions toward me or my family.

And none of the investigating we'd done had given us any proof. If anything, what we'd seen on the surveillance camera last night had only cast doubt on whether the story the guys had heard from Beckett's supposed employee was true.

I wanted to know what was really going on, and the man in front of me might know more than anyone.

"All right," I said carefully. "But you stay over there. And talk quickly." I turned my chair around so I could sit down on it.

Beckett didn't move from his position by the door. He ran his hand through his sandy hair, looking briefly uncertain—more uncertain than I'd ever seen from this confident man. Then he squared his shoulders and met my eyes again.

"The only things I kept from you didn't have anything to do with you or your family anyway," he said. "They aren't the kind of things I'd tell *anyone*, because of the trouble it could make for us. I do work for a business that's been in my family for generations. We do deal in real estate among various other things. But not all of those business dealings are strictly legal… Actually, quite a few of them aren't."

My chest tightened at that admission. I felt the need to say the words out loud, to put a clear label on what he'd just confessed to. "So, you're a criminal, then?"

Beckett gave me a small, crooked smile. "That's one way of putting it."

He hadn't even tried to deny it. I swallowed thickly. "And I'm supposed to believe that even though you're involved in all this illegal stuff, you had nothing to do with the crimes the other guys and I have been investigating?"

"Just because I'm a criminal, that doesn't mean I'm out to attack you—or that I go around hurting innocent people in general. I've always tried to limit the collateral damage from our activities as much as possible and to focus on victimless crimes."

My eyebrows shot up. An edge crept into my voice as I spoke. "And are you sure there really are crimes with no victims at all?"

Beckett inclined his head. "Okay, so possibly someone is always taking a minor hit. But there are plenty of victims from all sorts of technically legal business practices too, a lot of them way worse off and less deserving of their trouble than anyone affected by my actions."

"And I'm just supposed to take your word for it?"

He gazed back at me with the unflappable composure I'd always admired in him. "You know who I am, Maddie. I didn't tell you the details, but I didn't pretend to be someone I'm not either. Everything you already believed about the kind of man you knew is still true. Maybe you don't like the new details you've learned, but consider that my work also puts me in a position to do plenty of good for the people around me too. Like setting up that pro bono medical clinic, which is still in the works. I wasn't lying about that either."

My stomach knotted. He sounded so sincere—but how could I trust a guy who'd just admitted that most of his dealings were illegal?

"I'll understand if you can't accept this side of my life," Beckett went on. "I knew it was going to come out eventually, so maybe it was wrong of me to put off the confession. You don't have to decide whether we could continue our relationship right now, as much as I'd like to. But no matter how you feel about the kind of work I do, the more important subject right now is your father's murder. And I promise you—I swear on the entire family business and my life—no one connected with me had anything to do with that."

My mouth pulled into a grimace. "That's easy to say but not so easy to prove."

"It's always difficult, if not impossible, to prove a negative. I'm sure you know that from your studies." A fond note warmed his voice just for a second and sent a tingle over my skin that I didn't know what to do with. "Like I told you, I had no idea he even was murdered until yesterday. I've spent the past day verifying that my family wasn't involved. The 'proof' the other guys offered revealed my ties to some of the businesses you didn't know about, but none of those businesses actually factored into your dad's death, did they?"

They didn't. We hadn't been able to find any connection between Beckett and the places we actually knew Dad had been mixed up with. I sucked my lip under my teeth to worry at it.

"You did see me at the club before we met," I pushed, watching his reaction.

Beckett sighed, and for the first time a twinge of regret passed through his expression. "The first time I saw you, you were at the club with the other guys. I'd been keeping an eye on *them* for a few months because they'd been sticking their noses into the underworld of this city, and I didn't know what their end goal was. I wanted to make sure they didn't know anything about my operations that could harm my family."

A prickle ran down my back. "So you set yourself up to bump into me—so that you could find out more about them?"

"At first," Beckett said quietly. "But it became clear very quickly that if they were wrapped up in anything on my level, you didn't know about it… and also that you were more than worth pursuing simply for who *you* are. I didn't really *need* to talk to you again after that first conversation. I simply wanted to. I wanted to get to know you, and then I wanted to keep seeing you, only because of how much you brighten my life. You're something special, Maddie. And if someone's been threatening you, then I'll do everything in my power to stop them. I'm sure I can do a hell of a lot more than that trio of college boys."

He'd continued speaking softly the whole way through, but a thread of menace wound through his tone with the last couple of sentences. His back drew a little straighter, his expression hardening.

I was dealing with not just a criminal but a leader among criminals, and he was willing to put all his influence and power into defending me. It should have scared me, and it did a little, but at the same time I couldn't deny the thrill that shot through me at his intensity.

It took me a moment to find my tongue. I wasn't going to let him win me over that easily. "I still don't know that it isn't someone under *your* orders who was making those threats. It isn't just the club and the trucking company. The guys have direct reason to believe you're involved." I wasn't going to betray them by giving away what they'd heard and from who, not until we were sure it was safe to tell Beckett.

Beckett frowned. "Then they must have been misinformed by someone with a separate agenda—most likely, to cover their own tracks. I have to assume that whoever was responsible for your father's murder, it was another criminal who's aware of my family's dealings and saw us as an easy target to frame so they could divert your investigation." His eyes flashed. "Unfortunately for them, with my underworld connections, I can help you track them down. And see justice done however you'd like it served."

The dark promise in his words provoked another tingle that raced straight to my core. I glanced away, grappling with my feelings.

Everything Beckett had said made sense. It was a

much more reasonable story than anything the Vigil guys had been able to cobble together with the vague evidence and hearsay they'd had to rely on.

If Beckett was telling the truth, he could be the key to finding out what had really happened to Dad—and who had done it. How could I throw that chance away because of a sketchy stranger's words?

I had no idea how to wrap my head around everything he'd told me about his life. I'd been falling for him, hard, but the idea of dating a guy who was a consummate career criminal… I winced inwardly at the thought.

But then, was that reaction really fair? Beckett did illegal things, but how many times had I watched the Vigil guys break into buildings they weren't supposed to have access to and resort to violence to get their way?

They did it in the name of justice. Beckett's family used crime to make money. So maybe the ends justified the means in the Vigil's case. But I couldn't even say that Beckett's ends were all that bad if he used the profits from activities he claimed didn't hurt anyone innocent to set up places like that pro bono clinic.

I rubbed my forehead with the heel of my hand. He'd said I didn't need to decide how I felt about him personally or our relationship right away. That the most important thing was figuring out the crime that'd now affected all of our lives. And no matter how conflicted my emotions were about the things he'd admitted, I couldn't say I thought he was lying.

Between his story and the way the evidence added

up—or didn't—I couldn't see how he could be involved in Dad's death or the cover-up. It was much easier to believe that the guy who'd pointed the finger at him had been purposefully misleading us for their own gain. The stranger had put on an act to convince the Vigil guys, and they'd fallen for it because they'd already been uneasy about Beckett's presence in my life. He really had been a perfect target.

I dragged in a breath. "Okay. I'm not saying anything about what'll happen between you and me until I've had more time to process all this and see what happens next. But if you're ready to—"

Before I could finish accepting his offer of help, my dorm-room door burst open, slamming into Beckett's back. As he stumbled forward, Logan hurtled into the room with Slade and Dexter at his heels, all of them tensed with protective fury.

CHAPTER
SIX

Madelyn

Logan threw himself straight at Beckett. He slammed the other man's body into the wall behind the door with the full force of his massive frame and whipped a dark object out from the waist of his jeans. As he pushed the thing against Beckett's throat, the bottom of my stomach dropped out.

It was a gun. Logan was holding a pistol to the underside of Beckett's jaw, glowering at him with so much brutal fury my pulse stuttered at the thought that he might use it.

"Logan!" I burst out. "What the hell are you doing?" Where had he even gotten the gun? I'd never seen him or any of the other Vigil guys packing anything like that before.

Slade and Dexter had stepped close around me as if to shield me, Slade touching the small of my back protectively and Dexter looking me over as if checking for injuries. Logan's attention stayed focused completely on Beckett.

Beckett stared back at him, his jaw tight in the uncomfortable position but his expression cool. His voice came out shockingly steady. "I can tell you don't have much experience with that pistol. If I wanted to, I could take it from you and you'd be the one with a gun to your throat. But I don't want this to be a fight."

"Too late for that," Logan snarled. "What the fuck are you doing here? Maddie told you to leave her alone. We're not letting you mess with her head any more."

"So, what? You're going to kill me here in her dorm room?"

Logan gave him another shove, his hand clenched around the front of Beckett's shirt and the other holding the gun in place. "Fuck you. I *should* kill you after all the shit you've pulled, and now this."

"If we can't trust you to stay away from Maddie, how can we trust you about anything else?" Slade demanded.

Beckett's gaze slid to me and then the man at my side. I couldn't imagine how he was staying so unfazed, but then, who knew how many times he'd had guns pointed at him before?

"She needed to know the truth," he said evenly.

"She needed to know that I can help her figure out what really happened to her father."

"Bullshit!" Logan snapped. "You're trying to turn this around so you don't take the blame, when you're a lying piece of shit who—"

My nerves were jangling with apprehension, but I'd had enough. I pushed past Slade and Dexter and grabbed Logan's arm by the elbow. He flinched at the sudden contact, and my heart lurched at the thought of him squeezing the trigger.

"Stop, Logan," I said, unable to keep my voice from shaking even as I spoke as firmly as possible. "Put the gun down."

"I'm not dropping the only thing that will have this motherfucker thinking twice before touching you."

I grimaced at my stepbrother. "He wasn't touching me before either. He really did just come to talk. And after everything we've seen and what he said, I believe him that he wasn't involved in covering up my dad's murder. I don't think he wants to hurt me—he honestly wants to help."

Finally, Logan let his eyes meet mine. His voice came out only slightly softer than when he'd been talking to Beckett. "Did you invite him in here, or did he sneak in like a weasel and—?"

"It doesn't matter," I broke in. "I understand why he came. He knows more about the kind of people we're dealing with than any of us, including you. If we're going to find out who *has* been targeting my family, we need everything he can offer. Isn't that what really matters?"

Logan's gaze flicked between me and Beckett, his expression hard. "He's been playing you. You can't believe anything he says. He's fucking dangerous, and I don't want him anywhere near you."

I dug my fingers into my stepbrother's arm, wishing I could wrench his hand away from Beckett with a yank. "I'm not saying I totally trust him. I'm not saying I forgive him either. I'm just saying he's on our side when it comes to this investigation, and we could really use his help if he's going to give it."

"After everything he's done—"

My temper frayed. "Oh, please. You're in no position to rant about hiding things from me or treating me badly. Do I need to remind you how the last two years went down? And you're the one holding a gun on an unarmed man—a gun I'm going to guess you didn't get by any legal method? You're the only one who looks dangerous right now."

Logan's jaw twitched. "That's not the same. I'm *protecting* you."

"And so is he. Maybe he screwed up along the way, but so did you. I know Beckett—I know him a hell of a lot better than the rest of you, and you should know you can trust my judgment by now. His family wasn't involved in the murder, and Beckett has nothing to do with the cover-up. Whatever else he might be guilty of, those things aren't part of it. He's been framed, and we need to figure out by who, because they're our real enemy."

Logan growled and turned back to Beckett, prodding his neck with the gun. "I don't know what you said to her to pull the wool over her eyes, but—"

Dexter cut in with a clearing of his throat. "Actually… it's obvious he didn't hurt Maddie in any way when he came here. They must have been talking for a while for him to have convinced her, but he was still at the opposite end of the room from her when we came in. And we all know that the logistics don't add up as far as Beckett being responsible for the recent threats. We saw that last night."

Logan's head jerked around with a flash of betrayal on his face. "*You* think we should trust this prick?"

Dexter raised his hands, holding Logan's eyes for a second before his gaze darted away. "I don't think it would hurt to hear him out. I doubt Madelyn would have believed him if he didn't have a good explanation. If we can poke holes in his story, we will."

"Yeah," Slade said, glancing between us uneasily. "Maybe this has gotten a little out of hand. You are okay, aren't you, Maddie?"

"I'm perfectly fine," I said sharply. "Thank you for finally checking instead of assuming I'm a damsel in distress." Then I let out my breath in a huff and gave Logan's arm another tug. "You don't have to trust him. Just hear him out."

"He broke into your dorm. He forced this

confrontation. He doesn't deserve to take another fucking breath."

For fuck's sake. I let go of Logan to fold my own arms over my chest, glaring at him. "I don't remember inviting the three of you over either, but you seemed to think it was fine to come barging in. I've had enough of this alpha bullshit. If you don't lower the gun right *now*, I'm going to call Campo and tell them you're threatening someone with a weapon. How do you think that report is going to look on your academic record?"

An incident like this would probably get him kicked right out of the school. Logan stared back at me, but I refused to budge. When he didn't answer in the first few seconds, I pulled out my phone.

"Fucking hell," Logan barked. He pushed away from Beckett and lowered his gun hand, keeping the pistol out but at his side. I could tell his muscles were tensed to whip the weapon up again if Beckett made one wrong move, but the other man stayed where he was by the wall, tensed but utterly composed at the same time.

"Thank you," Beckett said quietly. "I understand why you felt that approach was necessary. I'd want to do the same thing if I thought someone was going to hurt Maddie. But I promise you, I only came here to clear the air and set things right."

Logan snorted in disbelief, but he seemed to have run through the worst of his rage. I jumped into the moment of silence before he could start shooting off his mouth again.

"We need to work with Beckett to keep this investigation going—and to see it through before anyone *else* gets hurt," I said. "We clearly don't have enough connections to put together the pieces on our own, and it must be someone on Beckett's radar, or they wouldn't have targeted him as a scapegoat. Although we're lucky he still wants to help out after the way you just attacked him."

Beckett tipped his head to me, his mouth twisting for just a second. "It's all right. I *have* screwed up; I'm not blaming anyone for being angry or having trouble trusting me."

Logan glowered at him. "All that smooth talk with nothing to show for it yet."

"Shut up," I told him without much real rancor. "You haven't given him a chance to show anything."

Dexter rubbed his chin. "No matter who we're getting information from, we have to continue the investigation with a lot of care. When these people have found out that we were getting too close, they've lashed out: first Madelyn's mom, then the Vigil office. I don't think we'd want them to realize that we're working with Beckett—or that we're continuing to investigate at all."

"My people know how to keep a low profile," Beckett assured him. "Now that we know what kind of a situation we're in, we won't let anyone see anything we don't want them to."

"Your people?" Slade repeated with a skeptical air. "What are you, the leader of the CIA now?"

Of course the Vigil guys didn't understand just how

well Beckett and his people could handle themselves in the criminal underworld. For all they knew, Beckett's family was simply involved in a few dirty local businesses and that was the end of it.

I swallowed thickly and squared my shoulders, bracing for the less-than-positive reactions I anticipated to come. "Beckett, I think you'd better tell them the whole story like you did with me. About who you are and what you're involved with. They're not going to understand until they've got the full picture."

For the first time since the guys had burst in, I caught a flicker of uncertainty in Beckett's gray eyes. He didn't like the idea of exposing his darker dealings with the guys. But he only hesitated for a few seconds before exhaling in a rush.

"You've uncovered a small portion of my family's business dealings. We have a long history in this area and throughout other parts of the country—and quite a lot of our activities are not entirely legal. And along the way, we've naturally made some enemies."

CHAPTER
SEVEN

Madelyn

"I don't think my family has ever done business in this town," Beckett mused as he drove toward the hospital in Logan's and my hometown. "I've never even been here before."

"Then bringing you was a useful decision," Logan said with a sarcastic edge.

I kicked the back of his seat. "Whoever has it in for Beckett *and* my family targeted my mom here. Beckett knows who his people have clashed with. He'll be able to recognize signs that could point to the culprit that we wouldn't notice." Then I glanced at Beckett. "We'll be at the hospital in a minute. If you want to drive around while we're inside, you can go and see if anything in this area gives you some ideas."

"You're just going to let him leave us high and dry without a ride?" Logan muttered.

I kicked his seat again. "Can you stop being an asshole for two seconds so we can make some progress here? He's trying to help us. It's his car."

Beckett held up one hand in a pacifying gesture. "I'll wait nearby just in case you two need to make a quick exit. I'd like to get the data sent off to my friend as quickly as possible anyway."

Logan scowled. "Your criminal friend who knows so much more than a doctor would."

"Doctors already looked over Maddie's dad's symptoms and test results, and they couldn't put the pieces together," Beckett said mildly. "My friend has a lot of experience with toxins and the ways they can affect the body, especially those that can be used to create the appearance of a natural illness. If there's any progress we can make from having a better idea what killed him, she's the one who'll get us there."

"Assuming we can get his records without a hitch," Logan grumbled.

Only with Beckett would my stepbrother downplay his own computer prowess for the sake of taking a dig at the other guy. I rolled my eyes at him even though he couldn't see me where I sat behind him. "I'm surprised you hadn't already grabbed his file when you hacked into the hospital system before."

"I looked at it," Logan admitted, "but it was obvious none of us in the Vigil could have made any sense of the data. We don't have any medical training.

And at the time I didn't have the skills to rip the files right out of the network without setting off red flags in the system."

"Well, this should be easy enough, grabbing them right from the source." I rubbed my hands together, hoping my confidence wasn't misguided. My heart was already beating a little faster at the thought of the deception I was going to be a part of.

Beckett drove past the hospital parking lot and pulled over to the curb a couple of blocks away. He wasn't coming in with us because we didn't want any of the security cameras catching us together. He'd picked us up away from campus too, in case we were being monitored there.

We didn't want our common enemy realizing that their gambit to frame Beckett had failed and we were now combining our efforts.

He glanced back at me as he turned off the engine, and I gave him a nod I intended to be reassuring. I still wasn't sure how to relate to him after the secrets he'd revealed. Keeping my mind on the mystery of Dad's murder was easier than figuring out what would become of the relationship we'd been building.

I picked up the manila folder I'd brought as part of my cover story and got out of the car. Logan hopped out to join me, and we hurried back toward the hospital.

"I guess we'll see if this friend of his is half as good as he claims," Logan said under his breath.

I elbowed him. "You don't have to be such an ass to

him. He didn't have to help us at all, especially after how you went after him. His connections *are* better than what we had access to on our own."

"If he's telling the truth about them," Logan said, and frowned. "And don't think I don't realize why he's really helping us."

"What's that supposed to mean?"

"He's still after you."

I shook my head. "You can't be pissed off at him for supposedly using me for his own ends *and* for really wanting to date me. It's either one or the other. And you shouldn't really be pissed off at him about the whole dating thing anyway. Last time I checked, that wasn't a crime."

My stepbrother settled for an inarticulate growl in response to that point, which was fine, because we'd reached the side entrance to the hospital.

As I reached for the door, Logan caught my hand. He pulled me to a halt and forced me to meet his eyes. "Be careful, okay?"

"All I'm doing is chatting up an old friend of my father's," I reminded him. "You're the one doing the risky part. *You* be careful. Don't bother with anything other than getting the record and getting out of there."

"Yes, ma'am," he said in a lightly teasing voice, and bent down to give me a quick but sweet peck on the lips. We couldn't afford to indulge in more than that.

This entrance was the closest to the research area of the hospital. We tramped up the stairs to the second floor, and then I went on ahead. Logan would be keeping watch to see when I'd cleared the way for him.

I walked along the row of offices, sharply aware of the door to the one that had used to be my dad's as I passed it. The name on the plaque was different now, of course, but I'd visited him here enough times as a kid to remember.

Rebecca's office was just a couple of doors down. She'd worked with Dad when he'd been alive and taken a few minutes out of her day to talk to me the last time I was here. I was counting on her being willing to pitch in on my behalf again. That way we'd know one office was definitely empty so Logan could get into the computer network from there—and I'd keep her busy until I was sure he'd retrieved the file we needed.

The knowledge of the deception left me queasy, but I ignored the sensation as I knocked on Rebecca's door. She opened it a moment later, and a smile spread across her face as she looked at me over her glasses. "Madelyn! It's lovely to see you again. Was there something I could help you with?"

She was so genuinely pleased that the smile I'd thought I'd need to force came naturally. "I'm in town to visit my mom, and I was really hoping you'd have some free time as well. I'd love to pick your brain about a research project I've been working on in school. I'm sorry I didn't call ahead—I wasn't sure how to contact you. I don't suppose you have time today? Maybe we could chat on your lunch break?"

I'd purposefully shown up around noon to make

that offer as easy to accept as possible. Rebecca paused for a second to consider and then nodded with another bright smile. "I think it should only take me another minute or two to wrap up what I was in the middle of, and then I was just about ready for a break anyway. If you don't mind the cafeteria food, we can talk down there."

I sighed in totally unfeigned relief. "That would be perfect. Thank you so much."

In no time at all, we were walking over to the elevator to travel down to the cafeteria. "Tell me about this project," Rebecca said as the car whirred downward.

I forced myself to focus on the project I really was working on for school, one her expertise could be of some use for, and not what Logan might be encountering upstairs while I kept her distracted. Or my guilt over causing that distraction.

"I'm looking at inherited diseases and how they can interact with contagious illnesses to exacerbate existing conditions," I said. "Chronic health conditions are one of your main areas of research, right? I was hoping I could bounce some ideas off you about which interactions would give me the most material to investigate—where there's the most data and that sort of thing."

Rebecca's eyes lit up with scholarly interest. She hummed to herself as we stepped off the elevator and headed into the cafeteria, where a rich savory smell told me that pasta with marinara sauce was the day's special. "I can definitely point you in some good directions.

That's a fascinating subject! Complex, but I'm sure you're up to the task. You're your father's daughter, all right."

She flashed a smile at me, and I smiled back while tamping down another flare of guilt.

"I try," I said, grabbing a premade salad from a display to keep up appearances even though I wasn't really hungry. "I figured getting your advice would help me hone my research."

I didn't want to talk about Dad. Ideally I'd like to avoid having him come up again in the entire conversation. If anyone listened in on our chat, they shouldn't get the slightest impression that this was anything other than an academic endeavor. No investigating happening here.

Please, let Logan find what he was looking for without getting caught.

Rebecca got the pasta, and we sat down at a table in a quiet corner to dig in. In between bites, she mentioned a few different conditions and the illnesses they often coincided with, and I tapped many hasty notes into my phone.

Getting her thoughts really was giving me a lot of ideas about the direction I'd want to take. I just wished I wasn't pulling one over on her at the same time. Every bite of salad stuck in my throat.

If Logan *did* get caught, she'd realize I'd been manipulating her. The thought of how she'd look at me then, the way her smile would crumple, sent a jab through my chest. I wrenched my mind back to the comment she was in the middle of making, plastering a renewed smile of my own onto my face.

I was almost finished with my salad and Rebecca was halfway through her pasta when a text alert popped up on my phone. It was Logan, simply saying, "See you soon!" An innocuous message designed to let me know he'd finished the job in a way that no one else would recognize meant more.

My shoulders relaxed, a little of the tension in my gut unwinding. I dismissed the text and gulped down the rest of my salad, not wanting to take up too much more of Rebecca's time after she'd already given so much.

"Thank you," I said when she finished her current line of thought. "This has been so helpful. I'm definitely going to incorporate some of your suggestions into the project. I'm excited to get started on it now."

Rebecca beamed at me. "I'd love to see the finished report when you have it all written up."

We said our goodbyes, and I headed out, trying not to feel as if I had a mark of shame branded on my back. No one had any idea that I'd come here with nefarious intentions. And they weren't really nefarious when it was all in the name of finding Dad's killer, right?

As I hustled through the halls to the side entrance and out into the early afternoon sunlight, my stomach knotted with the thought of another person I hadn't really done right by—someone who deserved honesty from me way more than even Dad's former colleague did. Looking around at the streets I'd walked and driven along with my best friend beside me, I couldn't shake the sense of uneasy resolve that gripped my heart.

Logan was already in the car when I got there, back in the front passenger seat. He rolled the window down a little as I came around beside it. Beckett peered at me from behind the wheel, examining my expression.

"It all went smoothly?" I asked Logan.

"Simple as anything," he said, sounding a little more at ease than he had when we'd arrived. "I've saved the file to a couple of different backup servers and also passed it on to Beckett for his 'friend' to look over."

Despite the slight edge he gave to the word "friend," the two guys didn't appear to be in imminent danger of murdering each other. My hand dropped to my phone in my pocket. "Good. There's one more thing I want to take care of quickly before we leave. Give me a few minutes."

At their nods, I ambled a little farther down the street. I didn't want to have this conversation in the car with them listening in, and I knew by the time we got back to campus, I'd end up wrapped up in the mystery again. I couldn't give Summer the explanation I'd promised her just yet, but I had to at least make sure she knew how careful she had to be.

To my relief, she picked up on the second ring, though her voice was rough. "Maddie. I was wondering how long you'd leave me hanging this time."

I winced. "Hey. I'm so sorry. There's just been so much going on—"

"I know, I know. But what kind of stuff? What the

hell is going on with you, Madds? This isn't like you at all. You've got to fill me in."

I swallowed hard. "I want to. I swear it. And I'm going to when *I* know the whole explanation, okay? I'm still working on that."

My bestie let out a huff. "Is Logan messing with your head again? You can't cover for him, you know."

"It's nothing like that," I insisted. "I just—I've seen some things that've made me worried. I want you to be careful, all right?"

"Careful? What are you talking about, Mads?"

"Like—don't go out with anyone you don't know, and try not to be on your own when you do go out. Keep an eye on your surroundings, and get out of any situation that feels at all off."

I could practically hear Summer's eyebrows arching. "Okay, you're kind of freaking me out now. What have you seen? You're not on drugs or something, are you?"

I sputtered a laugh. "No. No drugs. I can't really get into it. I just—" I scrambled for a reason that would make sense. "I've been a little paranoid after my mom's accident. It was just a freak thing, and I feel like it could happen to anyone, you know? I'll just feel better if I know you're being careful."

"Sure, Maddie. I don't want to end up in a car accident or anything like that either. You know I'm not exactly a wild child anyway."

No, but Summer wasn't a wallflower either. She enjoyed being bold and assertive. Hopefully my warning would sink in enough to make sure she recognized it if there was a moment when running away was the better option.

"I know, I know. It just makes me feel better to talk to you about it. And I should be able to fill you in on the rest soon. You take care of yourself."

"Maddie—" Summer started, and my throat constricted. I didn't know what else to say to her.

"I've got to go. Talk soon!"

I hung up, feeling twice as shitty as before. Had I done enough to protect her? How could I possibly know that?

All I could do was hope to hell that my warning hadn't even been necessary.

CHAPTER
EIGHT

Dexter

The hotel on the outskirts of town didn't look like much, the dingy, white-washed bricks in need of a fresh paint job and a lone employee in the small lobby who gave me a bored look. She said nothing as I strode down the hall as if I belonged here, following the directions Beckett had given me.

Our theoretical ally had said this was a neutral location, and Logan hadn't dug up any sign of a personal connection to the place. We'd arrived separately and discreetly to ensure it wouldn't be obvious we were meeting. All the subterfuge had me feeling like I'd stepped into a spy flick, which was both unnerving and a little exhilarating, if I was being honest. None of our work as the Vigil had ever gotten quite this complex.

My role was to fill Beckett in on the pieces of the puzzle we'd put together so far. It was easier not to be noticed going alone, and we'd agreed that I had the clearest grasp of all the moving parts in the conspiracy we'd gradually been uncovering. Besides, if Logan had come, he'd probably have been throwing Beckett against another wall within a few minutes. I wasn't sure Slade was feeling that much friendlier toward the guy.

I couldn't say I was totally on Beckett's side, but I could keep a clear head. I'd ask my questions, make my observations, and come to a conclusion about how he'd factor into our lives based on evidence rather than emotion. It was evidence that mattered more than anything right now, after all.

A plain sign saying MEETING ROOM 1 labeled the door I was looking for at the end of the hall. I pushed inside without hesitation and found Beckett already sitting at the eight-seater table inside.

He looked out of place amid the worn furnishings and the air that smelled like stale coffee someone must have spilled on the floor weeks ago. I'd always noticed he took care with his appearance, but maybe because today he was here in a business capacity, he'd donned a full suit, perfectly fitted, and combed his hair neatly back. He stood smoothly with an air of total professionalism.

"Dexter," he said in greeting, and started to extend his arm. But before I could indicate that I wasn't much for handshakes, he caught himself and switched to simply lifting his hand in an informal wave.

So, he'd noticed that I wasn't much for physical contact, just from our brief previous interactions. He was a sharp guy—I'd give him that.

I dipped my head in return and took a seat across from him. "I've brought everything useful from our files. But first I have some questions."

Beckett offered an easy smile as he sank back into his chair. "Straight to the point. I appreciate that. Just a second—a quick precaution." He tapped on the screen of his phone, which was sitting on the table, and it started playing a white noise track. To muffle our voices if anyone tried to record us, I realized. Probably unnecessary, but a simple protective measure.

Or maybe he was wary that *I* might be recording him for the Vigil's purposes.

If he distrusted me, he didn't show it. Beckett leaned back in his chair and spoke just loud enough for me to hear him over the hiss of static. "Ask away."

I rested my hands against the edge of the table, gathering my thoughts. I knew what I wanted to ask, but really all those questions were beating around the bush, trying to get at the one thing I couldn't ask directly.

The Vigil had already ended up veering down such a dark path—and I'd been the one who'd set us on that course. I couldn't let Beckett and his criminal dealings drag us even farther down. If I got the chance to save us from ending up in a worse place, I had to take it.

My friends deserved better.

The impression of calm authority that Beckett maintained did relax me a little. Whatever he was involved in, he clearly wasn't erratic or unhinged about it. But that didn't mean it wasn't dangerous.

"You told us a little about your family's activities," I said. "I'd like to know exactly what sorts of business you're involved in. As many as you're willing to say."

"Sure." Beckett folded his arms loosely over his chest. "I think I mentioned that one of our main focuses is real estate flipping and property management. That's all legitimate. We also have a stake in several casinos and our fingers in the stock market."

I lifted my eyebrows slightly. "And your not-so-legitimate businesses?"

"Those we maintain at least a degree of separation from, if not more. Any gangs or other organizations operating in our territory kick a portion of their earnings back to us. We don't exert much control over what they do, but if we find out they're involved in any areas we disagree with, like human trafficking and specific drugs, we intervene."

"And you don't participate in any illegal activities directly?" I said, not bothering to hide my skepticism.

Beckett chuckled. "I shouldn't make it sound like that. We always have front men, but we take a direct interest in some revenue streams from gambling, stolen and counterfeit goods, and extortion. Higher level targets, of course. People who can afford to lose."

I supposed those people had more to give up in

profits anyway. None of this sounded particularly horrifying, if I could believe him. It *was* pretty hard to imagine the man across from me sending people off on murder sprees or anything like that.

"You have some connection to that trucking company," I prodded.

"Yes. They're one of the businesses within our domain, answering to us, paying our tithe, and occasionally providing services."

"Are they involved in the criminal side of things?"

"Some of their clients have them ship illegal goods," Beckett admitted. "We've occasionally gotten rare alcohols that need to be smuggled in for the club through their connections, for example."

I pulled out the document with the trucking company logo on it and slid it across the table to him. "We picked up this report—I'm guessing now that it was planted as part of the effort to frame you. Most of the data is in a code I couldn't crack. Do you have the key to it?"

Beckett took a moment to study the papers and then tapped on his phone again, writing out a text. "I can get it. What's your number?"

I blinked, startled, and then rattled it off. In less than a minute, my phone pinged with an incoming text. The image that came with it was a page from the Bible, of all things, with one of the line numbers circled.

Instantly, my puzzle-honed brain latched on and

started unraveling the code from there. I held out my hand, and Beckett passed the document back to me.

The previously nonsensical strings of letters formed words in my head as I scanned the paper now. It was simply a list of dates, all of them from a few weeks ago, and locations that shipments had been dropped off at. Nothing unsettling there. They didn't even mark which deliveries might have been of stolen or otherwise illegal goods and which were legit.

"Thank you," I said after I'd finished my inspection. My nerves had settled some more, but there was one final gnawing question at the back of my mind. I forced myself to hold Beckett's gaze for a beat longer than I generally found comfortable before letting my attention shift to his forehead and then his cheek, where I could still judge his reaction. "If we find the person responsible for murdering Evan Silver, what are you going to do about it?"

"*When* we find him," Beckett said without hesitation, "I'll take care of it."

"Meaning?"

"Meaning you don't even need to worry about what I mean. I'll make sure they're never in a position to harm anyone else again. I'm not going to drag you, your friends, or Madelyn into that mess. You won't have to be involved, and you won't face any potential consequences. I'm the one best equipped to deal with the situation, and I know it isn't the kind of thing you'd want to be mixed up in."

He spoke coolly and firmly, and I found I didn't

doubt his honesty for an instant. It mattered to him, seeing this brand of justice done… not so different from the kind we dealt out as the Vigil. And he wanted to protect us and Madelyn from it.

How could I see him as a threat after that?

I leaned forward, my doubts satisfied, and took my laptop out of my shoulder bag. "I want to make sure it really is a 'when' and not an 'if,' so I've brought all the information we've gathered. It hasn't gotten us far enough, but maybe combined with your resources, we'll get some real answers."

I talked him through the full timeline, starting with Logan's realization that there was something questionable about Madelyn's father's death three years ago and our early investigations, then getting into the theft of Madelyn's car and the new directions that event had pointed us in. As I spoke, I brought up photos I'd taken and video footage from our surveillance cameras on the computer screen. I mentioned the bar where we'd found the trinket box, the old warehouse where we'd been attacked by security guards, and the seafood market that seemed connected to it.

Beckett took it all in silently other than occasional hums of acknowledgment. He studied the images I brought up on the screen with total focus, his mouth gradually curving into a frown. Now and then, he typed notes into his phone. As I got into the finer details, he started asking questions to clarify.

"What's this Baldwin file that comes up a few places?"

"We don't know," I admitted. "It seems to have been meaningful to Mr. Silver, but we haven't been able to locate it or to figure out who the name refers to."

"And this flyer from the seafood market is relevant because…?"

I could starkly remember the horror that'd gripped Madelyn's face when she'd seen it. "Madelyn says her father was babbling while he was sick—he sounded delusional. He said something about how a broken catfish had 'done this'—as in made him sick. Madelyn thought he was referring to an actual fish during a flood that'd happened a little while before, but when she saw the market's logo, she realized it was probably that instead."

Beckett's gaze darkened. "He'd made it that far through the chain of connections, then."

"Presumably. We don't know what he found out there or what the shipments passing through the market might involve." I watched him as he peered at the screen for a little longer and then added to his notes. His whole expression was shadowed now with a sense of gloom I couldn't remember seeing from him before. "Can you make anything of this that I haven't mentioned? Do you know who might have framed you?"

Beckett sucked in an audible breath. "I have some possibilities I need to look into, but nothing definite. I don't want to put ideas in your head until I've had time to confirm them. Thank you for going over all of this with me. I can tell you've been very thorough." He paused and turned his penetrating gaze on me. "Is Madelyn going to continue staying in your apartment for the time being?"

My hackles immediately came up. "She's a lot safer with us than in her dorm building—as *you* proved just a couple of days ago. We're not doing it to keep her away from you."

He held up his hands in a pacifying gesture. "Don't get me wrong! I'm not complaining about it. I *want* her to stay with you—I'm concerned about her safety too. And the three of you have shown that you take that very seriously." A bit of a smile came back, curling his mouth at a wry angle.

"We do," I confirmed, eyeing him for any sign that he was only faking his acceptance.

"And protecting her matters a lot more than who's spending the most time with her. Not that she's all that enthusiastic about one-on-one time with me at the moment anyway." Beckett shook his head ruefully. "I have a few trusted employees patrolling the campus surreptitiously when she'll be there for classes, but I can't cover everywhere she could possibly go. I'm glad she has the three of you watching over her as well."

I couldn't detect the slightest hint of a lie in his tone or his words. My stance relaxed. I didn't know if Madelyn would ever fully trust him or how I felt about him becoming part of our joint relationship again, but any doubts I'd had about how much he cared about her had vanished.

He understood how important she was. And if he

was going to put his criminal affiliations to use defending her, then I wasn't going to argue with that.

"We appreciate any steps you're taking to keep her safe too," I allowed, though I wasn't sure that "we" really included Logan. It was hard to say he appreciated anything about Beckett right now, even if I was starting to believe he probably should.

"She doesn't deserve to be stuck in this mess," Beckett said, standing up. "I'm going to do everything I can to get her out of it as quickly as possible. I'll be in touch as soon as I have any definite answers."

His face had gone tight again. He gave me a tip of his head and then marched out of the room as if in a hurry to start up his own investigations right now. Not quite the same coolly collected professional he'd been when I'd first come into the room.

Dread wound around my gut. What could this long-time criminal have noticed in the evidence I'd shared that would have made even *him* visibly worried?

CHAPTER
NINE

Madelyn

The smell of herbal incense drifted through the new age shop. I eased past shelves packed with crystals, essential oils, and other objects I'd never have come browsing through for myself. This wasn't my typical scene, but the place had seemed like my best bet in the city for finding what I was searching for.

"Hi there," the cashier called brightly from behind the counter. "Can I help you with anything?"

I paused, scanning the room, which was so packed with its narrow wooden shelves that it was hard to make out anything that wasn't directly in front of me. "I'm guessing you carry tarot cards—where would I find those?"

"We have a wide selection of decks on the back wall. Let me show you."

She led me over to the far corner of the shop. There had to be at least a couple dozen decks on display, but as I scanned the boxes, I didn't spot the one I wanted.

"There's a specific deck I was hoping to pick up," I said. "I don't see it here. Do you ever order things in specially?"

"Sure, as long as we can get it through one of our suppliers. What's the name of the deck?"

I grimaced. "I'm actually not sure. But I've seen the image on the box—the same as on the back of the cards. If I could look through an online catalog or something, I might be able to identify it."

The cashier gave me a kindly smile. "I'm pretty familiar with the options out there. If you describe it to me, I could probably figure it out without too much trouble."

As I followed her over to the counter, I dug through my memories of seeing Logan working with the deck. "The box was kind of a silky black. The top had a silhouette of a woman with her hands raised and her hair flowing out on either side—just line art, silver and not very detailed. The same image was on the backs of the cards but not shiny there, more of a pale gray."

"Oh!" The delight in the cashier's voice gave me a jolt of hope. "That's a more obscure deck, but I've always liked that one. I'm sure our main supplier carries it. Let me just see how long it'd take to get them in.

And I'll let you take a look to make sure it's the right one."

"Thank you," I said with a rush of relief.

The woman tapped away at her computer and then swiveled it so I could check the image on the screen. A smile stretched across my face with a lifting of my spirits. "Yes, that's exactly it. I can get them?"

"Definitely. It should only take a few days before they arrive. You can leave your phone number, and we'll send you a text when they're in."

"Perfect. Thank you so much."

The cashier beamed at me. "It was my pleasure. Thank you for stopping by!"

I walked out of the store with the sense of a small weight lifted from my shoulders. It wasn't a lot, but at least I'd made progress on one of the many problems that'd been nagging at me lately.

My victory gave me a boost of confidence. I had other problems to tackle—and I might as well get on with doing that now. It was only a phone call, but my stomach knotted up every time I thought about it.

I was going to have to lie to my mom again so that I didn't have to tell her the real reason I was asking questions about her and dad's old life together.

I dropped into the driver's seat of my car and leaned back, willing myself to relax. Then I pulled out my phone and dialed Mom's number.

"Hey, hun," she answered in a breezy tone that set me even more at ease. I couldn't hear any hint of lingering pain still coloring her voice. She really had set the car accident behind her. "Is everything all right?"

I let myself give a soft laugh. "That's what I was going to ask you. I just wanted to check in and see how you're doing." Lie number one.

"Oh, you shouldn't be worrying about me. I'm doing great. You've got enough on your plate with school and the rest."

She had no idea how large "the rest" actually was. I swallowed thickly. "It's easier to concentrate when I know for sure you're recovering well. Anyway, this has been a bit of a slow week for school." Lie number two. I didn't want to keep counting.

"Have you been working on anything particularly interesting these days?" Mom asked with a rustle that told me she was moving around the room as we talked. Maybe doing chores, maybe assembling pieces for one of her scrapbook projects.

"I have a new project on interactions between chronic diseases and contagious ones," I said, remembering my conversation with Rebecca. "It's bringing up a lot of information I didn't know before. And genetics is always fascinating—how much gets decided before we're even born."

"I find it so hard to wrap my head around any of that. I'm glad you have more of a mind for science."

"Yeah." Not that my mind had been all that focused on it lately. I thought of the lab reports I'd dashed off and the lectures I'd only half listened to and winced.

Mom would be the worried one if she knew how distracted I'd gotten.

I jerked my mind back to the subject I'd really wanted to talk about. "Have you been keeping busy while you're healing? Lots of friends dropping by to check in on you?"

"Oh, yes, I've had a few visits and offers to help. One of the benefits of small-town life." She chuckled. "Not that there's anything wrong with living in a bigger city, but I do like that close-knit feeling."

I strained my mind to dredge up the names of family friends we'd seen fairly regularly when I was a kid. We had no reason to believe that whoever had targeted my dad had known him personally, but we didn't know it *hadn't* been someone close to the family either. They'd figured out what he was up to somehow. If any of Mom and Dad's friends had faded away shortly after his death, that would be worth looking into.

"Do you still see the Brylers these days?" I asked. "Joanne and… I don't remember her husband's name?"

"Oh, dear, I haven't thought about them in quite a while. They moved out to Connecticut a few years ago. Or maybe it was Colorado." Mom paused. "Somewhere starting with a C. I doubt they even heard about the accident. But Maureen and Joe stopped by with a casserole, if you remember them. Their daughter's just finishing her first year of high school."

I vaguely recalled a plump woman with curly red hair and a little girl I'd had to barricade from my room for fear she'd tear into my toys. I guessed that wasn't something anyone needed to worry about these days.

"That's great." I groped for another name. "There was that couple down the street you and Dad used to get together with now and then too, wasn't there? Stacy and Kyle?"

"Yes, of course. I'm impressed that you remember. They were always fun to spend time with."

My ears perked. "Were? You don't see them anymore?"

"No, not in years."

"Was there any particular reason? Did you have a fight or something?"

I could hear the frown in Mom's voice. "Well, no. I can't even think of what it was. Sometimes people just drift apart, you know."

It felt too pointed to specifically ask if it'd happened right after Dad's death. "I can't remember the last time we saw them…" I said, attempting to prompt her.

"Neither can I. Oh, but I remember they came by with a cupcake for you when you graduated from elementary school. That was so sweet of them."

My interest deflated. I'd graduated elementary school a couple of years after Dad's passing. It didn't sound like that couple had pulled back specifically around that time. But if they'd already started to fade, it could be related, I supposed.

Mom's voice took on a puzzled tone. "Why are you so curious about them? Is there something else on your mind?"

I clenched my jaw for a second before pushing out another lie. "No, I guess I just got caught up in thinking about that close-knit neighborhood we had. Everyone is a lot more distant here in the city."

That line of questioning had pretty much been a dead end. Thankfully Mom gave me an out all on her own. "I hope you're not getting lonely out there. You know you can call me whenever you like, but make sure you're going out to the college social events and that sort of thing too. It can take some time adapting to a transition. I should let you go so you can get on with that."

My mouth twisted into a bittersweet smile. "I'll do that. It was good talking with you, Mom."

After I'd hung up, I sent a quick text to Beckett. That one couple probably had nothing to do with Dad's death, but they'd slipped out of Mom's life soon enough afterward that it couldn't hurt to alert him. I had to feel like I'd accomplished *something*.

I want to hear all the details straight from your mouth, he wrote back. *I have some news too, and it's better not to have much of this written down anyway. Meet me at the park where we grabbed ice cream the other day?*

I hesitated, but the truth was, I didn't feel at all worried about my safety around Beckett, no matter what shady business activities he was involved in. He might be a criminal, but I knew he didn't want to hurt me.

I just wasn't sure how far I could trust him outside of pursuing this investigation together.

When I reached the park, I spotted Beckett waiting in the shade of a tree a short distance down the path that led to the ice cream shop. He tipped his head to me, the wind ruffling the leaves and his sandy blond hair, and a pang shot through my chest.

Just a week ago, I'd have stepped right into his arms and enjoyed a kiss. Would we be able to get back to that easy intimacy?

Would I *want* to?

To his credit, Beckett didn't push for anything more than a conversation. He walked a little ahead of me on the path and turned off it into a secluded clearing where I found a bench surrounded by enough trees that it wouldn't be visible to anyone passing by on the path. He sat down at one end, leaving plenty of room between us when I sank down at the other side.

"You think these family friends could have been involved?" he asked, pulling out his phone.

I shook my head. "It's a long shot. I just want to cover every possibility. They were pretty good friends with my parents, and they drifted out of my mom's life not too long after he died. Probably just normal life changes, but there's a tiny chance guilt played a part."

"Names?"

"Stacy and Kyle. I don't remember the last name, but they lived on the same street as my parents' house for several years—they may still be there. Hopefully that's enough for you to trace them?"

"Absolutely." He shot me a mild but warm smile

and tapped the information into his phone. When he looked at me again, the intensity in his gaze brought to mind his passionate touch when we'd run back to his car out of the wind the last time we were here. A flush crept over my skin despite my best efforts.

"You said you have some news on your end too?" I asked quickly as a diversion—and because I did want to know.

Beckett's mouth twisted, so I knew it wasn't anything all that good. "I heard back from my poison-expert friend. Anthea's pored over your dad's medical records, and she's found a few hints that suggest foul play. But there's nothing overt enough for her to even be sure of exactly what toxin was used. Whoever was responsible, they covered their tracks very thoroughly."

My heart sank. "So there's no evidence we could use to prove the case in those reports, then."

"Not with just the hospital records. They may help us connect the dots to other proof we turn up. And it tells us we're dealing with someone who's both skilled and meticulous."

"Wonderful," I grumbled. "Anything else from the other things you were looking into?"

Beckett hesitated, his gaze lingering on my face. "I've made a little progress, but I'm still sorting through all the information."

"Is there any way I could help with that?"

"Maybe," he admitted. "But, Maddie, I don't want to put you in any more danger than you already are."

Hearing him use my nickname with all the familiarity of our past relationship tugged at my heartstrings, but the rest of what he said sent a prickle of irritation through my nerves.

"It's my dad we're investigating. I want to be involved as much as I can." I narrowed my eyes at him. "Logan tried very hard to push me out when my car got stolen, and that didn't go his way. I don't recommend you take the same tactic."

One corner of Beckett's mouth quirked upward. "You have always struck me as a woman who goes after what she wants—and generally gets it."

"Well, there you go."

He spread his hands. "It isn't just you, though, is it? The more you're involved, the more chance there is that the people we're working against will realize and strike out not just at you but the people you care about again."

My thoughts slipped back to my conversation with Mom, and my chest tightened. "I don't want that. Isn't there anything I can do from behind the scenes, things that aren't likely to get noticed? The sooner we crack this case, the sooner we'll all *really* be safe."

"You do have a point there." He tipped his head to the side in contemplation and then met my eyes again. "I can think of one thing you can do that shouldn't put any spotlight on you. It's a small help, but it could lead me straight to the person who tried to frame me."

I sat up straighter with a jolt of eagerness. "What? Let's do it."

Beckett let out a soft laugh. "I'll have to get a few things set up first, but we should be able to give it a try tomorrow." His hand twitched as if he'd considered reaching toward me and then thought better of it. "I really do admire how dedicated you are—to this cause and everything else you're doing with your life. And that bravery, being more than ready to jump right into action no matter what we might face. I never lied about how much I liked that side of you either."

A lump rose in my throat. My gaze dropped to my hands as I fumbled for the right response while his praise tingled through my veins.

It was so easy for him to talk like that. Just like he'd made himself seem like the perfect Prince Charming when we'd first met. But there was so much more going on behind that polished front.

But he'd given me what I needed in the ways that mattered most too. I lifted my gaze to meet his again. "I appreciate that you're letting me be an equal part in this situation instead of shunting me off to the side for my supposed protection. It means a lot."

The gleam in his eyes sent off a fresh flare of heat through my body. "I've always seen you as an equal, Maddie. I know you're more than capable of holding your own. If I *can* protect you and the people you're close to from the worst parts of my life, I'm going to do that, but I'll be upfront about it the whole way through. You can count on that."

When he said it that way, I believed him. I

restrained a giddy shiver. "You said we can do this thing tomorrow?"

He nodded. "Let me know what time in the morning works best for you working around your classes, and we'll meet up then. I'll pick you up behind the theater downtown—and we'll see if we can catch at least one rat."

CHAPTER
TEN

Madelyn

The van had looked old from the outside, with smudges of dirt and patches of rust, but the interior proved that was just a disguise. I sat in the back on a bench padded with smooth leather while thin but soft carpeting rested beneath my feet. But the comfortable furnishings didn't stop me from squirming on the bench as the vehicle swayed around a corner with a rumble of the engine.

A moment later, the driver parked. We must have reached the seafood market. He glanced back at Beckett, who was poised on the bench across from me.

Beckett gave him a quick nod. With no further prompting, the guy adjusted the collar of his polo shirt uniform, grabbed a clipboard that was part of *his* disguise, and stepped out of the van.

We watched through the grimy windows as he headed over to a neighboring building and put on a show of theoretically inspecting the vents protruding from the brick wall. When I turned back to Beckett, he was watching me.

"Are you ready?"

I dragged in a breath. "Yes. Let's get it over with."

He handed me a burner phone and a slip of paper with a single phone number scrawled on it. The phone number that would give me a direct line to the store manager at the Fresh Catch Seafood Market.

"Do everything as we discussed," Beckett said. He'd gone over the plan with me the moment he'd picked me up behind the theater. The market was just opening for the day. The manager was definitely in, but he shouldn't be too busy yet.

There was nothing to worry about. Other than that we were pulling a con on someone who was probably connected to my dad's murderer.

The people involved in the crime would undoubtedly know my face. That severely limited how much I could help with any hands-on investigations. But this maneuver wouldn't be caught on any cameras, and the manager wouldn't know my voice. Beckett had come through with a way I could be a part of our mission to take our enemies down, just as he'd promised.

I tapped in the number and willed myself to breathe

slowly and evenly as the line on the other end rang. The words I was supposed to say whirled in my mind. I focused all my attention on the first sentence.

One thing after the other. It was no big deal, really. But the reaction we might provoke mattered a lot, in ways I didn't fully understand but Beckett was clearly equipped to deal with.

My pulse jolted at the click of the answered call. "Carl here, Fresh Catch Seafood."

My mouth moved automatically, the words I'd rehearsed spilling out. "Your next special delivery has been moved up by three days," I said, keeping my voice monotonous but firm.

The statement sounded strange coming from my mouth, but the manager inhaled sharply. "No, that can't be right."

"We expect the market to be ready," I went on, as if he hadn't spoken. As he started to sputter something about usual timelines, I simply hung up.

A tremor ran through my body as I sagged back against the side of the van. Beckett tipped his head to me approvingly. "You were perfect. I'd love to see how he's freaking out right now."

"*If* he's freaking out." But the guy definitely hadn't sounded happy. "And now…?"

Beckett was already setting a small metal box on his lap. Two cables connected it to a laptop that was open on the bench beside him. He flicked a switch and scooted even closer to his side of the van, which had been parked just inches away from the back wall of the market. Studying the data that trickled across the laptop's screen, he adjusted one dial and another before appearing satisfied.

"Now we wait for him to follow the bait."

"I didn't know you were a techie too," I said, raising my eyebrows.

He laughed. "I wouldn't know how to use this gadget without help. I got it from one of my friends back in Paradise Bend—a county I've spend a bunch of time in. *He's* the real techie, a tech genius really. He's brilliant at this stuff." Beckett paused and glanced over at me. "I'd bet in a few years, Logan could get to where Gideon is if he keeps working at it."

What would Logan have made of that compliment from the guy he'd been so hostile to? The lack of respect must have only gone one way. "You really think so?"

One corner of Beckett's mouth quirked up into a crooked smile. "I might not appreciate his attitude toward me, but I can recognize talent when I see it."

He checked the screen again and fiddled with the controls a little more. "This should pick up nearby cell signals, but I don't want the range to be too broad, or we'll catch people all the way over on the street... We just need to cover the market building, and maybe only the back. That's where the manager's office is. I don't think he'd make this call where the regular employees can hear—"

He cut himself off at an emphatic *beep!* from the machine. "Here we go," Beckett said, and tapped a couple of keys on the laptop's keyboard.

As I leaned forward, my heart thumping in anticipation, a voice I recognized as the manager's burst from the speakers with a faint hum of static. "—got a call about the special deliveries. I don't know how they even had my number! Aren't you supposed to deal with this stuff, Sharply?"

The voice that answered sounded much more collected, low and cool. "When did they call? What exactly did they say?"

"It was just a few minutes ago. They said… something about the delivery being moved up. That the market should be prepared for it. I don't remember exactly. I was thrown off by the whole thing."

"It would have been helpful if you'd paid more attention. Did you recognize the voice?"

"Of course not! I've never talked to them before. It was a woman—that's all I know about it. She didn't give a name, obviously." The manager let out a huff.

The other man's voice turned even flatter. "You don't seem to have very much information to go on."

"That's because this isn't my thing, Sharply," the manager snapped. "You're supposed to handle all this shit. You need to talk with them and sort it out. And tell them you're the one they deal with, not me. I've got a business to run here."

"So do we. But I'll look into it. Go back to your spreadsheets and order forms, and you'll hear if anything needs to change on your end."

The other man sounded almost bored by the exchange, but the manager was so flustered I knew it was a big deal. These 'special deliveries' couldn't be legal, right?

The call cut off with a crackle, but Beckett was grinning. His fingers clattered over the keyboard before he clapped his hands together in satisfaction. "I got the number for the outgoing call. We're going to track this bastard down—Sharply, it sounds like his name is."

A fitting name for someone who killed people. But who knew if this was the kingpin or one more step up a long ladder. The people we were up against seemed to deal in all kinds of layers of subterfuge.

It got us closer to answers, though. "Sharply isn't a common name," I pointed out, my spirits lifting a little. "That should make it easier to narrow down who it was."

"Let's hope so. It could be an alias—but even that will be useful with my connections." Beckett pulled out his phone. "I'll pass the information on to my own tech team to see where it takes them. We should be able to follow this thread to whoever's in charge."

He didn't think the Sharply guy was, then. I guessed it wouldn't make much sense for a criminal mastermind to be the contact person for store managers at their front operations.

But the farther we worked our way up the chain of operations, the closer we'd get to the people who were truly responsible for destroying my family—and attempting to destroy Beckett as well.

He must have sent a text to our driver too, because a moment later, the man in the false uniform returned to the driver's seat. Without a word, he started the engine and pulled out of the alley behind the market.

I rested my hands on the warm leather on either side of me. "Where are we going now? I have the whole morning—are there other ways we can prod information out of these people?"

"I think we've covered all the ground we can for the moment," Beckett said, and hesitated, holding my gaze. "But I was hoping we didn't have to end things for today like this. There's something I'd like to show you."

I tensed automatically, but there was nothing about the suggestion to provoke any concern. Beckett's expression remained mild if hopeful. He'd stayed on the other side of the van the entire time.

I bit my bottom lip. "What would you be showing me?"

"I'd rather it was a surprise. I don't think it'll mean much until you're seeing it. But if you're uncomfortable, I can drop you back off by the theater instead. It's up to you. I realize you might not fully trust me still."

He wasn't pressuring me. He'd been giving me plenty of space all along. And he'd kept his word in everything he'd said he'd do so far, including letting me have a hand in tracking down Dad's killer today.

If I didn't give Beckett the chance to show whether he was worthy of more trust, how would I ever know whether we could rebuild what we'd once had?

I wavered for a second longer and then said, "I trust you enough to come along for the ride. Let's see this thing."

CHAPTER
ELEVEN

Madelyn

The van pulled to a stop outside a large building that was all gleaming glass and steel. Beckett opened one of the back doors and offered his hand to me to help me step out.

When he shut the door with a thump, the engine thrummed and the driver set off again. I wondered what instructions Beckett had given him.

Through the broad front windows, I could see that the rooms at the front of the building were empty, no furniture or decoration. As Beckett motioned for me to follow him up the front walk, I glanced over at him. "What is this place?"

"Part of my family business. I wanted to show you around."

He fit a key into the double doors and tugged the door open. I hesitated for a second before walking inside.

Light streamed down all through the entrance way from skylights high in the arched ceiling. A set of escalators that weren't yet running led up to the second floor, while a plaza with marble tiles and sleek columns stretched out beyond them, with windowed commercial spaces on both sides. A few already had signs mounted over their entrances.

Beckett strolled through the plaza at a relaxed pace. "I told you we'd bought a new office complex. This is it. We have plenty of legitimate business endeavors, and places like this are a big part of that side of our work. This is only our most recent purchase. Every company that sets up shop inside will be one hundred percent above board."

His pride in the acquisition rang through his voice. Then he stopped and pointed to one of the office spaces that filled one corner at the back of the plaza. The sign over top read, SMITHSON MEDICAL CLINIC.

"I'm still planning on setting up the pro bono clinic we talked about," he said. "That wasn't any kind of gambit—no matter what you think about me or how our relationship ends up, I really do want to give back to the communities we operate in. It shouldn't be all take. We've got a major sponsor on board, so the wheels are in motion."

My heart lifted, taking in the space. That office already had some furnishings set up: a row of padded chairs in the front waiting area and a broad front counter that would serve as a reception desk. I could easily imagine people in need settling into those chairs, filled with relief that they could get their problems looked at by a proper doctor without having to worry about going bankrupt.

"I don't think most criminals worry about how much they're taking," I couldn't help pointing out.

"We aren't most criminals. I'm not out to ruin people's lives. This community has helped support us in ways they don't even realize, and I think we have a responsibility to return the favor when we can."

Those were pretty words, but as I studied his eager expression, I couldn't ignore the twist of my gut. He couldn't present himself as a champion for good, not with the other things I knew about him now.

"If you feel that way, why do you get involved in anything on the criminal side at all?" I had to ask. "Why not go completely straight?"

A shadow crossed Beckett's face. He swiped his hand over his jaw, which had tensed as if he wasn't sure he wanted to answer that question.

Something tensed inside me too. I might have walked away right then if he hadn't started talking.

"I didn't exactly tell you the full story when I made my confession," he admitted. "I mean, everything I did tell you was true, I just didn't get into the full scope…"

I gave him a pointed look. "I think you'd better do that now."

He dipped his head in acknowledgment. "What I'm

part of, it's a family legacy going back generations. We aren't a normal criminal organization. We're one of a small number of crime lord families who control essentially all organized illegal activity around the world. The businesses we have a direct stake in are vastly outnumbered by the operations we oversee and monitor all across the globe."

I blinked at him, my voice failing me in the wake of that revelation. "All around the *world?*" I managed. Just who was this guy I'd thought I'd known?

But when Beckett turned his pensive gaze on me, I still saw that guy—assured, thoughtful, calm, and still with that glint of pride in his eyes.

"It's my heritage," he said. "I can admit that it's a challenging one, and not one I'm always happy about, but I feel like I've gotten pretty damn good at what I do. There aren't many CEOs or presidents out there juggling as many responsibilities as I need to on a daily basis."

"But... so much of it *must* be hurting people. If you're involved in that much of the crime around the world—if you've got that much power—why don't you *stop* it instead of keeping it going?"

Beckett's mouth slanted into a crooked smile. "It doesn't work like that, Madelyn. There are a set number of families who divide up the territory between them. If I pulled out or started trying to shut down all the operations in our domain, the others would find someone else to take our place. By participating, I *am* stopping some of the worst aspects of our legacy from continuing. I can moderate a certain amount of the criminal activity in this world to my own standards. If I backed away, who knows who'd fill that gap—what their priorities would be?"

I stared at him. It was impossible to wrap my head around dealing with those kinds of expectations and pressures. But Beckett had been born into it.

Had he ever really had much of a choice?

"It isn't fair," I said, my voice coming out quiet. "Just because you're part of one specific family, you have to take on this burden—"

He shook his head. "It's fine. It's *good*. I'm glad I'm part of it so that I can do what I need to. I've been in a position to prevent violence that would have happened otherwise, to save thousands of lives—I've made sure innocent people were protected when other forces meant to destroy them. I've gone against my own father..."

His words cut off as if his throat had closed up. He swallowed audibly, and I couldn't believe he was faking the flash of anguish that showed on his face before he regained his usual calm.

My own throat tightened. "That must have been hard."

"Yeah." Beckett ran his hand back through his hair. "There are power struggles sometimes, conflicts over turf. Dad jumped into one I didn't agree with, and things got bad, and... I wasn't going to just stand by and let the maniac working for him destroy a bunch of people who'd done nothing wrong, even if they were strangers. That's what I stand for."

There was no denying the conviction in his voice. It wrenched at my heart. I didn't understand what it must have been like growing up the way he had, with the expectations that'd been placed on him his entire life, the principles that'd been drilled into him that were so different from my own. I was judging him from my safe, peaceful, middle-class life, when I'd had no idea criminal organizations on the scale he was talking about even existed.

Would I really rather someone else was in his place? Someone who'd probably have less of a conscience than Beckett had shown he had in spades? I'd known plenty of people who were more selfish and vicious than he was who weren't even criminals.

I hugged myself for a moment, rubbing my arms up and down, and then let my hands fall to my sides. "I know you're not a bad person. I just—it's been a lot to take in."

"I get that." Beckett held my gaze for a moment, his eyes searching mine. Then he held out his hand to me, not looking like he expected me to grasp it but more as a symbolic gesture. "Come with me a little farther? I have one more thing here to show you."

I had no idea what to expect next. I trailed behind him, still absorbing everything he'd just told me, and he led me across the plaza to another office that appeared to be unclaimed. There was no sign up top, anyway.

Someone had been making use of the space, though.

Stepping inside after him, I found a small table with two chairs, the table draped with a white tablecloth and set with glasses, plates, and napkins.

Beckett bent down by a bar-sized fridge that was plugged in nearby and got out a few different trays of food: one a charcuterie board with sliced meats and cheeses, another with a rainbow spread of different fruits, and a third with three different types of sushi rolls. He laid them out on the table between the plates and poured sparkling lemonade into the glasses.

The tang of the beverage tickled my nose as I stared at the spread, my mouth watering and my mind whirling. "Is this some kind of picnic?"

He chuckled. "You could put it that way. I was hoping you'd have lunch with me."

He'd gone to an awful lot of preparation to set things up. A pang of affection reverberated through my chest. I cocked my head, unable to keep my curiosity in check. "What would you have done if I hadn't agreed to come with you after the phone call at the market?"

One corner of Beckett's mouth curved upward. "I'd have eaten on my own. Wouldn't want good food to go to waste. It was a gamble worth taking. But I'd rather eat with you, if you'll stay."

He pulled out the chair on his side of the table, and I rested my hands on the back of the one for me. Some distant part of my mind suggested that I should still be cautious, that I shouldn't let myself be convinced, but I couldn't summon even a particle of real fear about the man standing across from me.

He had a difficult life that he'd made the best of—that he was trying to do good things with. I could respect that. And knowing how much pressure rested on his shoulders, how much power he wielded not just in this city but around the world, made it all the more incredible that he was stepping away from those duties even momentarily to have this moment with me.

It was incredible that he *wanted* me. Who knew how many women he'd met in his line of work who were tougher and more experienced and more accepting of his career than I was? But I was the one he'd come back to.

Maybe he wanted me *because* I wasn't like the people he normally associated with. He'd said something like that before, hadn't he?

I slid into the chair, my heart thumping faster. I didn't know exactly what we were doing, but this felt an awful lot like a date. And maybe I was okay with that now.

"Sushi and charcuterie are an interesting combination," I couldn't help teasing as I helped myself to a few pieces of both.

Beckett grinned, looking more at ease now that I'd officially joined him. "I happen to be a big fan of both, and I see no issue with indulging in them together. Also, you mentioned to me on one of our dates that you haven't had fresh sushi in ages and you didn't care for the grocery store stuff much. This was prepared just a couple of hours ago by my family chef, who spent a few years training in Japan among other places."

I blinked at him and quickly raised one of the tuna rolls to my mouth to try it. The raw fish melted like butter as I sank my teeth into it, the rice breaking apart but not crumbling, faintly sweet. I gulped it down, my eyes widening. "Wow, that is good. Family chef, huh? One of the perks of your line of work?"

Beckett shrugged, his expression both amused and pleased. "I'll admit I'm not very handy in the kitchen, and neither is my dad. Having someone like that on staff ensures we stay fed. It's not an indulgence I'm particularly proud of... other than when I can use it to make a pretty girl happy."

I raised my eyebrows at the flirty remark. "And how many pretty girls have you had your chef preparing picnics for?"

Beckett's eyes smoldered. "You're the first. If I have my way, you'll be the only."

A quiver of heat raced over my skin, pooling low in my belly. I had to pop another roll into my mouth to stop myself from drooling—and not only over the food.

"What time is your first afternoon class?" Beckett asked.

I was about to rib him about whether he had even more plans for our time together when a generic ringtone pealed out... from my pocket.

My head jerked down. I stared at my hip for a second, trying to figure out why my phone would be making that unfamiliar sound, and then it clicked.

"It's the burner," I said with a hitch of my heart.

"The one I used to call the manager at the seafood market."

Beckett had tensed in his seat. "It'll be someone involved in this mess," he said in an urgent tone. "Answer it on speaker phone and see what they have to say."

I yanked the phone out of my pocket and hit the speaker button as I set the device down on the table between us. "Hello?"

My voice wavered just slightly. I inhaled deep to try to steady myself.

A baritone voice growled from the other end of the line. "I'd like to know who I'm speaking to and what business you had with the Fresh Catch Seafood Market."

Beckett's expression tightened even more with a twitch of his jaw. He made a cycling motion with his fingers, indicating that I should talk—and keep this man talking with me.

I groped for the right thing to say that sounded suitably criminal-ish for someone who'd have been making deals and arranging top-secret deliveries. "I could ask the same thing. Who are *you*?"

"I asked first, and I don't like people who play games. Identify yourself."

I gathered all the false bravado I could. "I don't see why I should have to. And I can do business with whatever stores I want. It has nothing to do with you."

The voice on the end crackled through the speaker, getting even harsher. "It has every fucking thing to do with me, and I think you know that. Cough up some answers, or you're going to regret it as soon as I get my hands on you."

Somehow I had the feeling I'd regret it even more if I did tell him who I was. I folded my arms over my chest, and Beckett waggled his phone at me. He'd typed out a sentence in his notes app for me to say, since he couldn't speak without giving away that he was here.

I read the line and quickly recited it, even though I wasn't totally sure what he thought it would accomplish. "I think we might even expand our association with the market. There's plenty to gain out of grabbing customer credit card information."

The man sputtered with apparent fury. "You can't be serious. Only an imbecile would bother with that kind of petty fraud." He let out a huff. "You're wasting my time. I don't know what you're up to, but I'll figure it out. And then you'd better believe I'll deal with you."

He hung up with a sharp click.

I let out my breath with a shudder, all my nerves jittering, and glanced across the table at Beckett. He was frowning at the phone, his expression gone ominously dark.

"Do you know who that was?" I ventured.

He grimaced. "I think I might." He shoved back his chair and stood up, contemplating our half-finished meal with regret. Then he pulled out his own phone. "I hate to abandon our lunch, but I should check a few things right away—things I can't look into from here."

My stomach knotted, but not because of the meal

cut short. I pushed to my feet. "I get it. This is way more important. Are you sure you'll be okay?"

Beckett nodded briskly, typing out a text as we hustled toward the complex's front doors. "I know how to deal with people like this." His gaze slid back to me, and his voice softened. "Before I get going, I'll have the van swing by and drop you off closer to the university."

I was dying to badger him with questions, but I knew Beckett well enough by now to realize that he'd tell me what was going on when he was ready. "All right. If the driver could let me out near the new age shop downtown, that would be perfect."

"I'll tell him that." Just a few steps from the doors, Beckett paused and touched my arm. "I'll be back in touch soon. Stay inside until the van comes around, and then walk straight to it."

"Okay." I wasn't going to argue when he was speaking so somberly.

He nodded to me and hesitated again, leaning toward me just a tad as if he were about to go in for a kiss. Then he squeezed my arm and yanked himself away.

I watched him stride down the front walkway, my spirits sinking. What could he have heard in the call that'd disturbed the most implacable guy I'd ever met so much?

CHAPTER
TWELVE

Logan

The damn code *wouldn't* run.

I'd gone through it well over ten times, trying to find the character that made the entire sequence invalid. It had to be a typo somewhere —something small and nearly impossible to find in the dozens of pages of code. My frustration had been progressively rising as I searched for the error, and after my twelfth—thirteenth?—time going through it, I still found nothing.

I knew why I couldn't find it, of course. Each time, I'd make it through a handful of lines of code, fully focusing, and then once I reached the end of the page, I'd realize that my mind had been elsewhere. On Maddie, mostly.

The project was important, and I had to turn it in by the end of the weekend, but nothing could top the danger she was facing. That was all I could think about, and it consumed every corner of my mind. What was a stupid computer science project worth when some murderous psychopath had Maddie in his sights?

What was any of the work I'd put in here at college worth when I couldn't guarantee I could keep her safe? What was the point in getting a degree, in setting myself up for a good job—what was the point in any of this if I lost her?

Finally, I pushed myself off the sofa and stalked around the apartment's living room as if I could outpace my worries. My hand automatically reached for the pistol I'd stuffed in the back of my jeans. The feel of it in my hands—the warmed metal, the solid weight of it —settled my nerves just a fraction. It was something concrete I could put to use if Maddie was threatened.

At least, until I remembered the panicked expression on Maddie's face when she'd seen me pull it out and aim it at Beckett. She hadn't been prepared for that. *I* hadn't expected to ever handle an illegal firearm… but after her mom's accident and the fire in the Vigil office and then finding out Beckett had been lying to our faces, I'd felt worse *not* having a weapon that could match the kind any of those criminals could pull out.

Thank God for our own criminal connections. I'd been able to arrange to get this through Darrel with just a couple of brief visits to his chop shop, and he hadn't even asked any questions. I didn't trust the guy farther than I could throw him, but he was reliable in very specific ways.

And as long as Maddie was okay, I wouldn't *need* to use it anyway. I simply had it just in case.

As I meandered through the living room again, running my fingers over the barrel, Slade strolled out of his bedroom with his backpack. He dropped it onto one of the kitchen stools and gave me an unusually contemplative look that raised my hackles before he turned toward the fridge and grabbed a bottle of water.

He opened it as he swiveled back toward me and chugged a few gulps. As he lowered the bottle, he tipped his head to me. "We'll get this whole thing sorted out, man. It's going to be okay."

A rough laugh burst from my throat. Of course he'd say that.

"Nothing about this is okay," I snapped before I could rein in my temper. "We have no idea what could come at us—or at Maddie—next. So don't pretend you know shit about it."

The second the words had burst from my mouth, shame prickled under my skin. My best friend hadn't deserved my anger. *He* hadn't done anything wrong.

But Slade wasn't easily fazed. Maybe he could tell I hadn't really meant the criticism. "I don't know shit about what's coming," he agreed easily. "But I know us. I know we won't back down until we've figured everything out and destroyed the threat. It's as simple as that."

He slung his backpack over his shoulder and headed out of the apartment. I watched him go, my stomach knotting. I couldn't get my assignments done, I couldn't talk to my friends like an actual friend… I had to get a grip, or I'd become a liability rather than any kind of hero.

I shoved the gun back into my jeans and flopped down on the sofa. I couldn't do anything about the assholes we were up against right now, so I might as well at least get this assignment off my plate. Surely I could locate one little error.

I'd barely had a chance to try when the doorknob clicked over. Maddie eased inside and shot me a warm smile as she closed the door behind her.

Relief flooded me at the sight of her. Her blond hair and sweater-and-jeans combo were unrumpled, her face bright. She'd gone off to do some kind of reconnaissance with Beckett against my muttered objections, but she hadn't come back any worse for it. If anything, she was in a better mood than she'd been in when she left.

Which probably shouldn't have irritated me as much as it did.

"Did you have a good time with the mob boss?" I couldn't help asking, even as I winced inwardly at the snark in my tone.

Maddie simply rolled her eyes at me, which was about what I deserved. "The point wasn't to have a good time. I think we made some progress. He acted like he had a lead, but he didn't want to tell me about it until he'd confirmed his suspicions." She paused, her gaze going momentarily distant with a crease in her brow, and then smiled again. "And I got to do an errand I've been looking forward to. I have something for you."

I blinked at her, thrown off course enough that I forgot my annoyance over Beckett. "For me? You didn't need to get me anything." A small pang resonated through my chest at the thought of her going out of her way to do something for me when she had so much else weighing on her.

"I know I didn't *need* to. I wanted to." She reached into her purse and pulled out a purple plastic bag. "I realize it can't make up for what you lost, not completely, but at least you can use them the same way."

She held out the bag to me. I took it and dipped my hand inside, registering the shape and size of the object with a tingle of recognition before I pulled it out. Then I just stared.

It was a deck of cards—of tarot cards. And not just any deck, but the exact same design I'd gazed at a thousand times on the back of Mom's old deck. The one that'd burned up in the library office fire.

My throat constricted. Maddie had been right, of course. They couldn't totally replace that old, familiar deck. They didn't have the worn corners where Mom's fingers and then mine had moved over them or the shiny star sticker on the bottom of the box that she'd let me stick there when I'd been a little kid. But they brought back so many of the same memories. It was almost as good.

The pang in my heart expanded into an ache that spread from the base of my throat to my gut. The sensation was bittersweet. There was grief at the thought of all the time I hadn't gotten with my mom and the connection to her I'd lost with the original deck, but also a swell of gratitude and affection toward the girl who'd gone out of her way to try to mend that loss the only way she could think of.

And it'd been a pretty great attempt. No one could have done better. Maddie had wanted to do this for me —had considered my pain that thoroughly despite everything she was dealing with.

I got to my feet and wrapped my arms around her, tugging her into the tightest of hugs. The floral scent of her shampoo filled my nose as I bowed my head next to hers. "Thank you. So much. You have no idea how much this means to me."

Maddie squeezed me back. "I can imagine. I just—I don't want to let them win. I don't want them to take anything more from us."

How the hell had I ever let myself push this amazing woman away? But as I held her close, an image rose up in the back of my mind of her leaning into *Beckett's* embrace instead—welcoming his touch, offering him affection. My body tensed up before I realized what was happening.

I pulled back, peering into her eyes. My voice came out taut. "How can someone who's as good a person as you be okay with what Beckett's admitted to? How can you even stand to be around him?"

A shadow crossed Maddie's face. She took a step away from me, the corners of her mouth pulling down. "Are you serious right now?"

I grimaced. "What? It's true. He's a fucking career criminal, and you—"

"Stop it!" Maddie interrupted, jabbing her finger at me. "Just stop it. All I wanted was to do something nice for you, and you had to turn that into another excuse to rant about Beckett? Do you hear yourself?"

I flinched. I'd just told myself I'd never push her away again, and then I'd turned around and done exactly that, if inadvertently.

"I just don't get it," I said stubbornly.

Maddie let out a huff, narrowing her eyes at me. "I'm still with you even though I've watched you break into buildings, hack into private databases to steal information—hell, you were even responsible for a murder that you covered up rather than going to the police about it! You know you did all those things— and who knows how much else that I don't have a clue about—and you're still a worthwhile human being. Why can't you accept that Beckett could be too?"

I gaped at her for a second, unspoken words clogging my throat. The ones that spilled out of me weren't anything I'd have wanted to say if I hadn't felt as if she'd socked them right out of me.

"I *don't* think I'm a worthy human being."

The second the admission was out, I longed to take it back. Maddie froze, staring at me.

"What do you mean?" she asked in a quiet voice.

A sense of hopelessness swept over me. It was out now. I couldn't pretend I hadn't said it.

I sank down onto the sofa and rubbed my hand over my face. My gaze focused vaguely on the wall across from me.

"I hardly think I deserve to be *alive*," I said hoarsely. "I got this second chance thanks to the liver transplant —because someone else, some other kid, died instead of me. I sure as hell didn't earn that. And my illness, even after the transplant, totally messed up my family. My parents were arguing a lot after I got sick and while I was recovering... They weren't really on good terms even when my mom died."

Maddie lowered herself onto the sofa next to me and clasped my hand. I let her, but I couldn't bear to look at her.

She twined her fingers with mine. "You have to know none of that was your fault. You were sick. You didn't have any choice in the matter. The kid whose liver you got would have died whether you needed the liver or not. And if the situation put that much of a strain on your parents, then their marriage wasn't that strong to begin with. That's not on you."

"I just don't see why I should have gotten to live and not someone else." My head drooped. "I've tried to convince myself that I've earned it by helping people as much as I can—finding things for them and getting justice when they needed it. But doing *that* has led me into all kinds of dark territory I can't say I'm really happy about... Why do you think I've worked so hard to shield you and everyone else I care about from who I've become?"

"Logan—"

I shook my head to cut her off. "It's fine if I end up getting hurt while I'm protecting people—helping people—the best ways I can. I've already gotten so many more years than I was originally supposed to. But I've got to draw the line somewhere. I don't want to see anyone getting caught in the crossfire."

With those last words, I sagged into the sofa cushions. My entire abdomen felt hollow, as if I'd been wrung out by my confession—all the things I'd never admitted to anyone out loud before.

What the hell could I say now? What could Maddie say to me? Now she knew just how fucked up I was.

But she didn't shy away. She scooted closer on the sofa and wrapped her arms around me, resting her head against my shoulder.

"Don't you know how many good things you've already done?" she said softly. "If you hadn't gotten a second chance, you wouldn't have been there in junior high to stand up to the kids who were bullying me. You made me feel that *I* was worthy of more, of being treated better—of demanding better for myself and everyone else."

I turned my head toward her for the first time, her

words wrenching at me. "Of course you deserved better."

She touched my cheek, holding my gaze with her gorgeous blue eyes. "You say that so easily for me but not for yourself. But—you think I'm so amazing? It was *your* confidence that inspired me to take more stands myself. I wouldn't be who I am without you in my life. And the darkness you've gotten mixed up in could be the reason we finally find justice for my dad. I can't believe there's anything wrong with that."

I couldn't argue away the conviction or the admiration in her words. It was hard to wrap my head around the picture of me she was painting, but there was no denying that Maddie believed it. And if she believed it, with that keen mind of hers and her unshakeable moral code, then who was I to debate the subject?

I pulled her closer to me, tucking her legs over my lap and nestling her head under my chin. She relaxed into my embrace, her body melding against mine as if there was no place else she was meant to ever be.

But that wasn't totally the case. There *were* other places she belonged—other guys she belonged with.

And maybe, if I absorbed some of her compassion and generosity, I could admit that it was possible Beckett was one of those guys.

He hadn't done a single thing to hurt Maddie, which was more than I could say for myself. If I looked over all our interactions and what Dexter had reported back after their meeting, it'd appeared he was doing everything in his power to protect her.

Maybe I'd been too hard on him because of how hard I was on myself, not because of anything definitively horrible that he'd actually done.

It was going to take time before I'd fully accept what Maddie had said, but my spirits lightened as I held her close. The space inside me no longer felt so empty.

If I could have cuddled there with her for the rest of my days, I thought I'd have been perfectly happy with that as my life.

But of course, I was never going to get *that* lucky. We'd been tucked together for maybe ten minutes when Maddie's phone pinged with a text alert.

She eased back just enough to retrieve it from her pocket. The screen cast a starker glow across her face.

"It's Beckett," she said, and tensed slightly as if in anticipation of another caustic remark from me.

A twinge of hostility rippled through me, but I let it pass. "What's he got to say?" I asked, keeping my tone even.

Maddie shot me a gentle smile that made my effort worthwhile before her gaze flicked back to the screen. Her forehead furrowed. "He says he needs to talk to all of us about something important. He wants to know if he can come over—he'll be discreet."

She glanced at me again, waiting for my answer. I dragged in a breath and acknowledged to myself what I'd been fighting so hard to avoid.

We needed Beckett and his resources. And maybe, just maybe, the woman in my arms needed him too.

"Sure," I said. "I'll call in Slade and Dexter. Let him know we should all be here within the hour to hear his big news."

CHAPTER
THIRTEEN

Madelyn

"Are we sure Beckett's coming?" Slade asked impatiently, tossing one of his cinnamon candies to the ceiling and allowing it to fall back into his hand as he lay sprawled across the sofa. "Maybe he's blowing us off."

I shook my head and snatched the candy midair when he tossed it again. I dropped it on the coffee table in front of me.

"I second that question," Logan added from the chair across from me.

"He said that he'd wait until everyone arrived so that we could get started right away," I reminded them. "He should be here any time."

Slade let out a huff that was half-heartedly

impatient. "He didn't tell you anything about this big news of his?"

I shook my head. "I'm guessing it's the kind of thing he wouldn't want to bring up on the phone."

Logan grimaced. It looked as if it took particular effort for him to say, "That does make sense."

My eyebrows just about shot right off my head. Logan caught my gaze and held it for a moment, and the memory of how we'd embraced on the sofa just an hour ago tugged at my heart. He'd wrapped his arms around me as if I were an anchor in a storm, the only thing keeping him from spiraling into disaster.

But he seemed settled now. I thought the things I'd said had dissolved the worst of his fears about himself and what he deserved. How could he think he wasn't even worthy of being *alive*?

Dexter shifted on his feet where he'd been standing by the window, leaning forward to peer between the blinds. "He's here."

I was too restless to stay sitting after that announcement. I pushed myself to my feet and hurried to the window in time to see Beckett closing the back door of the car he'd just gotten out of. It was a modest Kia, not the kind of car I'd ever seen him in before, but he had wanted to stay anonymous. I'd bet it was an Uber.

He'd taken other obvious steps to stay under the radar. Rather than his usual tailored business clothes, he'd donned a baseball cap and sunglasses, his leanly toned frame hidden beneath a baggy sweatshirt and jeans.

It only took a few seconds for him to stride to the building's front door and disappear from our view.

Dexter moved to the apartment door automatically, hitting a button when the entry buzzer sounded. I forced myself to sink back into my chair. There wasn't any point in all of us jumping on the guy the second he came inside.

At a firm knock, Dexter pulled the door wide. Beckett stepped over the threshold, his sunglasses in his hand now. He considered Dexter and the three of us around the living room in the space of a heartbeat, as coolly collected as always, and walked over to stand by the entertainment system where he could face all of us.

As Dexter joined Slade on the sofa, Beckett gave us all another assessing glance. He held himself with an air of such authority even dressed so casually that there was no mistaking the power he could wield.

How could I ever have failed to realize that he had to be a major leader, someone who pulled the strings behind innumerable operations? His dominance was etched in every particle of his being.

"What's this all about?" Logan demanded, brusque but to my relief not overtly hostile.

Beckett folded his hands together in front of him. "We have a lot to discuss. I'm sorry for the urgent meeting, but I didn't feel it was right to leave you all in the dark now that I know what we're dealing with. Or rather, who."

Slade had straightened up while the other guy spoke. He cocked his head, curious but also wary. "And who is that?"

Beckett took a deep breath. "To explain that, I have to tell you more about who *I* am and how I factor into the criminal underground. What I tell you today should not leave this room, or people who are much more vicious than me may see you as a threat to be destroyed simply for knowing."

Dexter studied him for a second with narrowing eyes before his gaze dropped. "That doesn't sound like a typical underground organization."

"That's because it's not. There's a group of thirteen families who call themselves the Devil's Dozen, and between them, they have influence over all the significant criminal activity that goes on throughout the world. My family is one of those. My father is the current head who generally meets with the other leaders, but I'm his heir, and I've already begun the process of taking over from him."

There was a moment of silence. The other guys simply stared at him. Then Slade let out a low whistle. "Fucking hell. You're some kind of black-market royalty —is that what you're saying?"

Logan's expression was more disbelieving. "All the crime in the entire *world*? That's not possible."

Beckett shrugged. "You can believe me or not. I've seen our empire in action. All that's important is you believe that I'm operating on a stage with only a handful of other major players who hold incredible sway, and one of those other players is directly involved in Evan Silver's murder."

My stomach lurched. "What? Why would any huge criminal king pin have it in for my dad?"

Beckett's gaze slid to me with obvious sympathy in his eyes. "I don't know that part yet. But this city is divided between territory belonging to my family, the Storm, and some that's part of a different family's empire: a man who goes by Doom's Seed."

"That doesn't sound ominous at all," Slade muttered wryly.

Beckett's mouth twitched with a hint of a smile. "He is a little over the top. But that doesn't stop him from being just as dangerous as his name sounds."

"What does he have to do with my dad?" I broke in.

"I'm trying to figure that out," Beckett said. "I only just confirmed that he's even involved. When I first found out that someone had been framing me and that Mr. Silver's death was connected to specific businesses in the city, I wasn't sure whether those were under Doom's Seed's control or part of some upstart criminal enterprise that was so new none of the Devil's Dozen had exerted authority over it yet."

My mouth had gone dry. "What we did at the seafood market this morning—was that to help you answer that question?"

Beckett nodded. "A man who has a definite interest in the shady transactions happening there is one of Doom's Seed's top lieutenants, Clarence Lindell. He's the one who called you up and tried to browbeat you. I was pretty sure I recognized his voice—and his attitudes about certain types of crime. A little digging confirmed his connection to the deliveries passing through the market."

I couldn't restrain a shiver, remembering the harsh voice that had threatened me.

Logan had tensed where he was leaning forward in his chair. "So, he's tied up in whatever illegal business the seafood market is handling. How does that tie him to Maddie's dad?"

Beckett aimed a baleful look at my stepbrother. "We know that Mr. Silver stumbled on something that made him a target. We know that whatever it was, it brought him to the seafood market and the warehouse that's also part of their delivery chain. We also know that someone with a lot of resources was able to set up Maddie's mother's accident and the fire at your office, as well as arranging evidence to frame me. It doesn't really make sense for it to have been anyone else."

I groped for my words. "Then we're assuming that this Doom's Seed guy had my dad murdered to protect his business. Whatever he found, it was part of this guy's dealings?"

"I'd imagine it's something like that," Beckett said, his voice softening. "It might not have even been Doom's Seed himself but his underlings handling operations for him that they don't think are important enough to run by him. Or that they don't think he'll approve of. I have trouble imagining them thinking coming at me was a good idea unless he'd either approved of it or they'd decided they didn't care what he wants."

"Maybe they've gone rogue," Dexter suggested.

"That's a possibility. Whatever the case, I'm going to confront the man in charge and tackle the problem head on."

Logan frowned. "And where do we come in?"

Beckett's jaw tightened. "You don't. The one thing we do know for sure is that Doom's Seed and his lackeys are incredibly dangerous on a level far beyond anything you've needed to deal with before. They have a thousand times more resources than four college students do, and it'd be much too easy for them to arrange a few more 'accidents' to dispose of you if they feel you're causing too much trouble again."

"They haven't come at us directly so far," I pointed out, though my heart was thumping faster.

"I think that's only because you've appeared to stop investigating," Beckett said. "And they'd only take measures that extreme if they believed they had no other choice, because it *would* look suspicious if something happened to all of you. But I don't know how long they'll hold off, especially if it becomes clear that you're still on the case."

He paused and swallowed audibly, the first outward sign of distress he'd shown since arriving. "I don't think I can fully protect you. I'm not even sure I can protect myself."

Those words punched a hole in my gut. I could hear

how much Beckett hated admitting it—how much he hated this whole situation.

"It isn't your fault," I had to say.

"It's not," he agreed. "But I'm tangled up in it now, and I'm *glad* that I am. I know how to handle these people—I've got by far the best chance of getting us all out of this situation alive and well, with justice served."

"What does that mean, exactly?" Dexter asked.

"I'm going to handle the entire investigation from here with my own people. The four of you should stay out of it—as far out of it as you can. Go completely back to your regular lives, whatever you'd have been doing if you didn't believe a murder had happened. That's the only way to ensure you won't become targets. I'll find out why Maddie's father was targeted and keep you all in the loop about everything I uncover. I promise you that."

Slade snorted. "You're going to take all this on your shoulders by yourself? Are you kidding me?"

Beckett's mouth curved into a tight smile. "I won't be alone. I'll have plenty of help—from my people, who've trained for this, who've dealt with Doom's Seed before."

"No fucking way." Logan shoved himself to his feet, his muscles flexing. "If you think you're going to steal our case out from under us after—"

"I'm not trying to steal anything," Beckett interrupted sharply. "I'm trying to keep you all *alive*. It's the only thing I know I *can* do."

Logan hesitated. Silence fell over the room again as the full impact of Beckett's stand sank in.

He was willing to take on all of the danger and the responsibility himself to avoid putting us at any risk. He'd rather go it alone than take the chance of backlash against us. Even though Logan had been tearing into him at every opportunity over the past several days; even though the other guys had viewed him with suspicion.

He'd told me he had a code of ethics, lines he wouldn't cross. That he tried to protect innocent people as much as possible. He couldn't have given a more concrete display of those principles than he was right now.

Maybe I didn't totally understand his way of life and how he justified it to himself, but any flickers of doubt I'd still had snuffed out. He might not be a good guy in all the typical ways, but he was more than good enough for me.

The same startled awe was crossing the other guys' faces. Logan opened his mouth, but I leapt in before he could say anything.

"No. You're not shutting us out."

Beckett gave me a pained glance. "Maddie, it's not like that."

I stood up like Logan had and set my hands on my hips. "However you want to put it, it's not happening. You want to protect all of us? Well, I want to protect *you* just as much. It's my dad. None of this would have happened if we hadn't been trying to unravel his murder. I'll be careful, but I'm not going to step back now and let you take all the heat. I'm standing with you, pitching in every way I can."

To my surprise, Slade got to his feet next, his expression tense but his eyes sparkling with determination. "I'm in this until the end too. It's our fight as much as it is yours. We'd be real cabrones if we let you march into battle alone."

Dexter sprang up too, his stance rigidly defiant. "I'm in. We stand together, all of us."

That left only Logan, standing there with his jaw working and turmoil in his dark gaze. He stared at Beckett for a long moment.

"I appreciate what you're trying to do," he said finally, his voice rough but genuine enough that relief washed through me. "You could have walked away from this whole mess and left us to deal with it, but instead you're doing the opposite. You insisted on pushing into our lives—well, now we're insisting on being part of yours. As far as we have to go, as long as it takes, no matter what hell we have to go through."

A tingle raced over my skin at the conviction in his words—and the knowledge that there really might be some kind of hell ahead of us.

Beckett gazed at all of us as if hoping we might change our minds. Then he sighed and rubbed his face. "Somehow I feel like arguing isn't going to get me anywhere."

I moved toward him and grasped his hand. "It isn't. Because we're in this together, all the way to the end."

CHAPTER
FOURTEEN

Beckett

watched the clock above the door as it continued ticking. Seconds turned into minutes as noon came and went, leaving me pacing the hardwood of the office floor.

He was late.

I'd requested a meeting with Doom's Seed at his earliest convenience, and today at noon was the agreed upon time. It wasn't in person, of course. Though I would have preferred that, he had denied the in-person invitation and countered with a video chat.

That was fair. Being a part of the Devil's Dozen awarded most people a level of anonymity. Nobody knew where he held a residence. He could have been in this country or halfway across the world.

Our jobs made it possible to live virtually anywhere.

Our jobs *didn't* make it impossible to join a damn video chat that'd been scheduled in advance on time.

I understood the game he was playing. It was the same sort of game that my father had played for years before his authority had dwindled. It was the same sort of game that I'd watched Mercy play so expertly in my time in Paradise Bend. Doom's Seed was intent on showing who held the power in this meeting, in this case by making me wait.

So far, he was nine minutes later than expected.

I hated playing into his desire for power and control. I had half a mind to disconnect from the video chat before he joined, walk off, and not be here when he finally got around to signing in. If it'd been any less pressing a situation, that's exactly what I'd do.

But if it were any less pressing a situation, I wouldn't have requested the meeting in the first place, and Doom's Seed probably realized that. If I wanted to keep Maddie safe, I needed to assess his involvement in the recent schemes I'd stumbled on. I couldn't turn back for the sake of my pride.

The clock hit precisely 12:10, and an alert pinged on my computer signaling that the other party had joined the video chat. I turned toward my desk and settled stiffly into my chair. As I put on a mild but firm expression for the camera, I approved his icon.

The man I knew only as Doom's Seed appeared on the screen. The plain beige background gave away nothing about his location, contrasting starkly with his typical flashy clothing.

In his usual garish fashion, he wore a vibrant gold-and-purple plaid vest over a shiny black button up with a tie that might have had actual gold thread woven into it in a paisley pattern. I restrained myself from rolling my eyes.

"Storm's heir," he said in greeting, with a sardonic tone that managed to make it sound as if he didn't think the title was earned. Not that he knew all that much about me. "My apologies for the delay. I had something important come up."

He didn't *sound* the slightest bit apologetic, which no doubt was purposeful. All the same, I treated the apology as if he'd meant it, not allowing the implied insult to affect me. It was better if I pretended I hadn't even noticed his subtle rudeness, though I kept my own tone brisk rather than placating. "I understand. Things come up. Thank you for coming."

I'd thought long and hard about how I'd structure this conversation. I had to be so careful with my words. Every conversation within the Devil's Dozen was a struggle for control, a fragile balance between maintaining authority and bargaining for what you wanted.

If I seemed weak, he'd consider it pointless to entertain my questions. If I outright challenged or insulted him, he might withhold the information I needed out of pride.

It was a precarious path with innumerable unpredictable obstacles.

Before I could begin, Doom's Seed cleared his throat. "Reaching out to a fellow member between official meetings over unestablished business is highly irregular. I trust you have a good reason for breaching typical protocol?"

"Of course," I said evenly. "Unfortunately, a matter has come up that couldn't wait. I recently discovered that one of your people has taken hostile action against me and therefore the Storm's empire as a whole. If you or one of your people are aiming to start a war on our territory, I don't plan on sitting back for weeks until the moon is right."

As I spoke, I studied his expression on the screen. His eyebrows rose slightly at my comment about war, but otherwise his face remained neutral. I willed my jaw not to clench.

If we'd been able to meet in person, I'd have had so much more body language to go by when evaluating his intentions. Communicating through a computer was an inadequate substitute. But it was all I had.

"I'm disturbed to hear that," Doom's Seed said as if he hadn't known already. He furrowed his forehead. "I was unaware that anyone who answers to me had acted against the Storm, and I'd certainly have wanted to know. What exactly happened?"

He was acting startled and confused, but not exactly upset. No one made it to the level of the Devil's Dozen without being good at subterfuge. Was his surprise an act, or had his lackey really gone rogue?

Not for the first time since I'd come back home, I wished I had Rowan here with me. Rowan was a master at reading people. He'd have picked up on more from the man across from me than I could.

But he wasn't here, and I needed to be able to make those judgments on my own.

I kept my gaze trained on Doom's Seed as I spoke. "I've been monitoring a group of college students who've gotten a taste for vigilantism. They've been investigating local criminal activities, recently some that appear to fall within your domain. One of your people tried to deflect those amateur detectives by claiming I was responsible instead. I'm sure you can recognize that the consequences of framing me, especially to civilians who might turn to the police, could be severe."

Doom's Seed rubbed his chin, looking thoughtful but still not particularly concerned. I hadn't mentioned anything about the ties I'd formed with the students in question or about the connection to Evan Silver, not wanting to show too much of my hand.

I'd hoped my adversary might give away some telling detail, but it was becoming increasingly obvious that he had an unshakeable poker face. My hands balled under the desk in frustration as I waited for his response.

He hummed to himself and gave me a look that felt irritatingly patronizing. "While I keep an iron fist with most of my people and operations, I give a certain amount of leeway for them to defend me as they see fit without informing me of every detail. It makes my underlings feel more comfortable in their positions. Less like I'll kill them for small indiscretions." His lips spread in a smirk. "It boosts morale."

I couldn't imagine anyone feeling all that happy working under the flamboyant brute on my screen no matter how much morale-boosting he did, but there was no accounting for taste.

"I would have hoped you wouldn't give them enough leeway to launch a turf war with one of your own," I said, letting an edge creep into my voice.

Doom's Seed gave a careless wave of his hand that only raised my hackles more. Whether he'd initiated the move against me or was only hearing about it now, he clearly didn't *mind* that his people had attempted to sabotage my family's business.

"It's possible whoever acted against you didn't even realize they were turning on a fellow member of the Dozen," he said.

I swallowed a snort. That was unlikely. I'd dealt with this specific lieutenant before—Lindell was perfectly aware of who I was and my familial connections. But harping on the issue would only make me look too easily shaken.

I raised my eyebrows at the man across from me. "Whatever the case, I trust you'll sort out the problem quickly and thoroughly, taking all appropriate measures to ensure it won't happen again? Or should we be prepared to deal out proper sanctions ourselves?"

Doom's Seed shrugged. "I'll tell my people to back off on anything directly to do with the Storm. But they aren't going to sit back and allow some kids to screw with my operations. If those 'vigilantes' impose on my dealings again, they'll face appropriate consequences too."

Was that meant as a threat toward me? *Did* he know that I was interested in that group of students from more than just the standpoint of caution?

I held my expression as implacable as his own. He might be testing me, checking to see whether I was invested in their fate. And if he knew that I was, I could turn them into even more of a target in the game he seemed to be playing.

"The students don't appear to be an issue anymore. Your men did a thorough job scaring them off. But of course you'll handle that matter however you see fit—as long as it doesn't impinge on the Storm's work."

"Naturally," Doom's Seed said, rolling the word off his tongue far too casually for me to believe he meant it. "Was that all you called on me for?"

I shaped my next question with even more care than the ones before. "Actually, there was one more matter I wanted to address while we're already speaking. A name has come up that seems to have some significance. Do you remember anything about a death about fifteen years ago—a man named Evan Silver?"

I didn't expect Doom's Seed to admit it even if he

did. I only wanted to see his reaction to my tossing the name out there without warning.

But I was dealing with a tough customer. Doom's Seed didn't show any sign of emotion other than disdain with the purse of his lips. "Do you know how many deaths I've heard mentioned in the time I've been doing this job, Storm's heir? Most of them are barely memorable. I don't recall even a fraction of the names. That one means nothing to me."

"I understand," I said. "I simply wanted to check."

His gaze veered to something beyond the camera, and his eyes narrowed. His attention flicked back to me. "You've gotten your time and presented your complaints. This conversation is over."

He didn't waste time for farewells before dismissing the video chat. I was left staring at a blank window.

I let out my breath with a brief growl. How much had I even learned from the attempt? I didn't think he cared what happened to me or my family's business, but he hadn't given away enough to convince me that he'd purposefully undermined us either. I still had no idea whether Doom's Seed had intended to move against us or if it'd really been only a lieutenant taking initiative he shouldn't have.

One thing was clear: Doom's Seed was no friend to the Storm, to the guys who called themselves the Vigil, or to Madelyn Silver. I'd have to keep an even closer eye on his people's operations in this city and their surveillance of the college. Things could take a much more dangerous turn so quickly.

As much as I admired Maddie's resolve and determination to find answers, I couldn't help worrying that we were all in over our heads—and we wouldn't find out just how much until the next unexpected strike.

CHAPTER
FIFTEEN

Madelyn

There was something warmer about our next meeting with Beckett despite the main circumstances that brought us together. We were perched on stools around the kitchen island, only Dexter standing as he moved between the island and the stove, where he'd cooked jasmine rice and a couple of different curries to fortify us for the conversation ahead.

I already knew to expect great things from Dexter's culinary efforts. Beckett hadn't sampled them before. As my first bite of the tofu and yellow peppers in ruddy sauce melted on my tongue, he brought his fork to his mouth. He chewed carefully, and his eyes widened.

"This is fucking good," he said to Dexter.

A broad grin stretched across Dexter's normally

subdued face. I had a feeling Beckett had just won a few points with the other two guys as well. There was no denying he meant the compliment, and the fact that I'd rarely heard him swear only emphasized his enthusiasm.

Slade stretched out his legs to the side of the island and scooped up another forkful of his own. "Yep, we're pretty spoiled around here. Dex has his place in the Vigil assured for all time as long as he can work a stove."

He winked at his friend, but something about his tone sounded a bit off to me. I couldn't put my finger on it, and my stomach twisted despite the delicious food.

It'd been too long since we'd really been able to relax and have a proper conversation with each other that didn't revolve around murderous criminals. I had no idea what other things might be on Slade's mind.

A small smile had touched Logan's lips, but he got down to business, waving his fork at Beckett. "This isn't a dinner party. What have you found out in the past few days? You said you were going to talk to that guy you think is behind this—Doom's Sprout or whatever."

"Doom's Seed," Beckett corrected him with a hint of dry amusement, but any sign of humor quickly faded from his expression. "I did speak to him. Unsurprisingly, he didn't launch into a full confession of wrongdoing or an overt declaration of war."

I frowned. "Did you get anything out of him?"

"Not directly." Beckett offered an apologetic grimace. "But it was a necessary step to make sure he knows he can't expect to hide his involvement. If he *doesn't* want a war, then he has to ensure his men stand down, at least when it comes to anything that interferes with my business."

"Wonderful for you," Logan muttered, and I aimed a kick at his shin.

Beckett appeared unfazed. "I do think I found out something else useful. I mentioned Evan Silver in passing at the end of the conversation. Doom's Seed didn't let himself react in front of me, but there's been a telling shift in behavior among his people since then."

Hope shivered through me. I leaned toward him with my elbows on the island. "What do you mean?"

"I've had my employees monitoring all of the companies the four of you connected to the theft of Madelyn's car, Mr. Silver's past investigations, and his death. Business was proceeding as usual at all of them until my conversation with Doom's Seed. It's been the same since at the chop shop, the bar, and the spa, but my comments must have spurred some changes at the warehouse and the seafood market."

Slade stopped chewing, his dark eyes lighting up with curiosity. "What kind of changes are we talking about?"

Beckett took another bite of curry before answering, as if he didn't realize the rest of us were hanging on his next words. Or maybe he did, and this was his way of heckling Logan right back.

"The warehouse from the address in the trinket box is now for sale through back channels. It looks like they're trying to offload it so it's no longer part of

Doom's Seed's holdings. And the man you had footage of regularly coming by the seafood market hasn't been back since then. Neither has the guy named Sharply who used to work there every other weekday."

Dexter came over to stand between Logan and Slade with his own plate. He set it down, his expression pensive. "What do you make of those changes? Do they point to anything we should be concerned about?"

"Not immediately," Beckett said. "But those two businesses were the ones already tied the most directly to Mr. Silver's death from the evidence we had. The fact that they're the only two where Doom's Seed has adjusted his operations confirms that they're a key factor, while the other businesses must not be all that involved. He doesn't want there to be any chance of you finding more proof of what happened back then."

My pulse stuttered. "Then this Doom's Seed guy is definitely behind my dad's murder?"

Beckett gazed back at me evenly. "It's too early to be sure. But either he knows the details, or he mentioned my comment to that lieutenant of his who could be making the changes independently. Either way, someone high up in the organization is moving to protect themselves."

"Then we need to dig deeper into those places," Logan said. "Especially the seafood market. It seems to have been some kind of hub for whatever they were moving around."

"The secret is in the fish," Slade said with a light laugh.

Dexter knit his brow. "It was the freezer container that led us to the seafood market in the first place. The thug who attacked Maddie was overseeing deliveries for them. We still haven't figured out what they're shipping."

"What would need to be kept cold over long distances?" I asked, tapping my fork against my mouth. "I guess it could be something edible—some kind of illegal food. Or—" The idea hit me with a jolt as I thought of the labs in the biology department where I spent so much of my class-time. "What if they're transporting bacteria or viruses for some kind of biological warfare? Or organic materials that contain toxins? Something like that is what killed my dad."

Beckett nodded slowly. "Something along those lines wouldn't surprise me at all. And it would definitely fit with the method of your dad's murder."

"Who the hell are they waging biological warfare on around here?" Logan demanded.

Beckett cut his gaze toward the other guy. "It can be on a small scale. Infect a small group that's in your way here or there. Or this is only the first step to transporting them overseas where there are plenty of wars being fought that you're barely aware of here in the States."

A chill ran through me with the knowledge that he was right. We could barely wrap our minds around the potential depths of this man's villainy.

This was the kind of person Beckett was standing in the way of when he kept his spot in the Devil's Dozen.

If he backed away, there might be no one working against the worst of the criminals—and another psychopath like this Doom's Seed psycho could take his place.

Suddenly it was hard to have any qualms at all about what he did, given the alternative.

Dexter hummed to himself. "That could explain how Maddie's father got involved in the first place too. They could be stealing samples from hospitals or other laboratories he did work for. Or he might have heard about a mysterious death that got him started on the trail. If he noticed something suspicious and then discovered the shipments, the criminals involved could have seen him as a threat."

"But why wouldn't he have told anyone?" Logan said with a little growl of frustration. "If he even suspected—he should have sounded the alarm, not gone digging all on his own."

When I gave him a pointed look, he made a face at me. "At least the three of us had each other for backup."

I guessed he had a point. But I could easily imagine why Dad would have kept quiet. "You should be able to understand his point of view, given how you've acted the entire time you knew. He must have realized he was onto something dangerous, and he was trying to protect me and my mom until he had something concrete he could bring to the police."

Logan hesitated. "I guess that does make sense. And it's hard to think of how he could have stumbled on any illegal materials these people are shipping that wouldn't be related to his work in the hospital. If we assume they're transporting biological samples or toxic substances, what would we need to look for next to prove that?"

In the moment of silence that followed, Slade pushed back his stool with a rasp of the feet against the floor. I realized with a start that he hadn't said anything in a while, just sitting there watching the rest of us hash out the possibilities. Like he was pulling back from the group.

"As much as my brilliant insights are solving both world hunger and global warfare, I've got to get to my study group," he said in a typically joking voice before I could ask if he was okay. "We've got an exam next week, and they'll all be lost without me. It'd look strange if I didn't show up."

We all nodded, but an ache formed in my chest as I watched him stride away. Something wasn't quite right with him, no matter how much he tried to pretend he was his usual jovial self. I didn't know how I could force him to talk about it, though. The next time I had him to myself, I'd have to bring it up.

As the door shut behind him, I yanked my thoughts back to the problem right in front of us. "I should try to get into more records at the hospital back home. I could look for any mysterious deaths or illnesses that came up there in the last few months before my dad died. Whenever he started writing those notes that you found about the investigation." I glanced at Logan. "If we figure out what tipped him off, that'd be a huge step forward."

"You don't need to be the one to do that," Beckett said. "I have people who can handle it."

I narrowed my eyes at him, understanding his protectiveness but unwilling to give in. "I have easy access to the hospital because my mom's still going back for check-ups after her accident. There'd be no reason for anyone to think it was strange for me to go back to visit."

"Doom's Seed might have people watching the hospital at this point. I don't like you putting yourself in unnecessary danger."

"It isn't unnecessary," I insisted. "I won't let anyone see me doing anything that'd be strange for a daughter helping out her mom. He'll be keeping an eye on you now too, won't he? Do any of your 'people' have a good excuse to stop by?"

Beckett's jaw tightened, but I could tell he didn't have a good argument for that. "We could get at it using a more roundabout approach."

"Which would take more time."

"Hey." Logan set his hand on my arm and, to my immense shock, tipped his head to Beckett. "He's making a reasonable point. *None* of us wants you in danger."

Because being overprotective was something that Logan could always relate to. I wanted to roll my eyes at the suffocating masculine energy in the room. "Of all the things you guys could have agreed on, could you pick something else?"

They both gave me a similar look that said, *Absolutely not.*

I glowered at each of them in turn. "Well, I don't want any of you in danger either, and I'm the one who'd be in the least. So I'm the obvious option." I paused. "Of course, there is the small problem that I don't know how to hack into the hospital network once I'm in the building."

The guys appeared to stew on that for a moment, Dexter shooting me a sympathetic glance. Then Beckett squared his shoulders. "Fine. I might know a way to help with that."

He looked at Logan, who hesitated before letting out a resigned sigh.

No more arguments. We were doing this.

We would make this work. With Logan and Beckett finally allied, there was nothing that could come between us and the truth.

CHAPTER
SIXTEEN

Madelyn

"Everything is healing well, Lindsay," the doctor said with an approving smile. "You've obviously been looking after yourself and keeping up with your physio."

Relief rushed through me. Mom kept her expression calm as she smiled back, but she squeezed my hand a little tighter where I'd grabbed hers while we waited for the doctor's assessment.

We both knew how bad her injuries from the car accident had been. She'd needed emergency surgery and been kept under observation for days. But now that she'd been home for a little while and was gradually getting back into her usual routines, it seemed she was recovering quickly. She had to be at least as reassured by that as I was.

"I've been doing my best not to be impatient about getting back to normal," she said with a light laugh.

The doctor nodded as he closed Mom's file. "Remember, strive for a *new* normal. Some of those injuries will likely be finicky for years to come. You want to continue being patient with yourself, and recognize that sometimes you may need to adapt rather than push through. There's no shame in that. But I think you'll get awfully close to that old normal eventually, if not all the way there."

"Of course. I'll keep that in mind."

He said his good-byes and left the exam room, and Mom sighed before getting to her feet and grasping her purse strap. The dejected sound made me leap up. "Are you okay?"

She swatted at me. "Yes. You heard the man! I just wish I healed as fast as a person half my age still."

"It hasn't been very long."

"No, not at all." She bumped her shoulder against mine affectionately. "You know, honey, you really didn't need to come. I'm used to attending appointments by myself."

"Not appointments like this," I said. "I'm glad I could be here when Holand couldn't this time. And before you say anything about concentrating on my schoolwork, it'll be easier for me to concentrate now that I've heard for myself that you're doing well."

Mom let out a teasing huff. "You know, usually it's mothers who attend doctor's appointments with their children, not the other way around." She paused as she slung her purse over her shoulder and gave me a more penetrating look. "You don't talk to me about school all that much anymore. You used to tell me about interesting lectures and projects you were working on all the time."

I feigned a laugh of my own. I hadn't had much to report because my mind had been so wrapped up in other things, and I'd been afraid that if I tried to fake enthusiasm where my heart wasn't in it, Mom would sense that something was wrong. It seemed like saying less might have given her that impression anyway.

We headed out the door and down the hall past bustling nurses and the beeping of machines from open doorways. "Oh, well, it's getting down to crunch time," I said. "My first semester at the new college, and final exams are looming. It's less exciting when you're scrambling to make sure you're stuffing your head full of every possible fact."

And worrying about your dad's murderer who nearly murdered your mom too, I didn't say.

Mom knit her brow. "Is that how you feel—like you're scrambling to keep up? I've never heard you talk about college that way before. You always seemed energized by the work rather than stressed."

"Oh, no, it's not that bad," I said, scrambling now to cover up the way I'd misspoken. I couldn't seem to remove my foot from my mouth with her today. "I'm exaggerating. But I am really busy, in a good way. You don't need to worry, I promise."

She patted my shoulder. "I want to make sure you're okay, just like you do with me." She peered at me again in a way that sent an apprehensive prickle over my skin. "You know that if you ever start to feel too stressed or uncertain about anything—school or otherwise—you can always talk do me, don't you? I'm here for you no matter what. I *want* to be here for you."

My stomach knotted. Where was this pep talk coming from? Had I been that bad at hiding all the stress that really was weighing on me?

I couldn't tell her the truth. Not when I had no proof yet. Not when the people I was trying to bring to justice had already left her with these injuries she might never fully recover from. She needed to stay as much out of this mess as I could keep her until it was all over.

"I promise that I'll come to you if I need your help. Pinky promise." I offered her a pinky.

A chuckle tumbled out of her as she grabbed my pinky and shook it.

"You never broke a pinky promise when you were little," she said, narrowing her eyes. "I expect the same now."

I gasped and placed my hand over my chest as if her words wounded me. "Have some trust. A pinky promise is permanent."

But I'd only promised to go to her if I needed *her* help, and this situation wasn't anything she could help with anyway.

Mom grinned, looking as if her momentary bout of worry had faded away. Which was good, because I had a trick to pull before we left the hospital, and the front doors were fast approaching.

We were just a few steps away when I stopped in my tracks and patted my pockets. "Shoot," I muttered, making sure to look at Mom and feel my pockets a second time as if double-checking. "I took my phone out back in the room to make some notes—I think I must have set it down and forgotten it. I'd better go grab it before someone else finds it. You go ahead. I'll meet you in the car in a minute."

"Oh, that sort of thing happens to me all the time. Good thing you realized before we left."

She waved me off, and I kept my game face on until I'd turned away. Even then, I restrained a grimace at my lie, far too aware of the hospital staff, patients, and visitors milling around the lobby.

I headed back the way we'd come as if I really were going back to the exam room, but I quickly turned down a different hallway—one with fewer patient rooms and more admin offices. It was almost lunchtime, which I hoped would work in my favor. I brushed my hand across the USB drive in my pocket, reassuring myself that it was still there, as if I hadn't felt it moments before.

I knew nothing special about computers and nothing at all about hacking, but I knew how to insert a flash drive. It would be hard to screw *that* up.

All I needed was to find an unmonitored computer

accessible enough for me to insert the drive. Beckett had said that the way his techie colleague had programmed it, the app on it would run automatically and insert the necessary code for our purposes in less than a minute.

I had to walk confidently and briskly as if I belonged here to avoid getting questioned by the staff, since there weren't many visitors wandering around in this section of the hospital. I picked up my pace when I spotted a nurse's station with a few computers up ahead, the chairs currently empty. My heart thumped faster.

Jackpot.

But just as I stopped on the opposite side of one of the desks from the computer, dipping my hand into my pocket and glancing around to see if I could lean over the counter to plug it in, a man in scrubs hustled into the station. "Can I help you?"

Shit. "No," I said, pasting on a smile. "I almost forgot the room number I needed, but it came to me the second I decided I had to ask. Isn't that always the way? Sorry to bother you."

"No bother at all," he assured me, but I hurried off with a false sense of purpose in case he watched me go.

Farther down the hallway, a woman strode out of a room, leaving the door ajar. Did that mean it was empty now? I slowed down just enough so that she'd pass me well before I got to the room and approached it cautiously.

I could see a computer on a long desktop just beyond the door. Was there anyone else in the room?

I rested my hand on the door—and a voice spoke from right behind me. "Were you looking for Beth?"

It took all my effort not to jump out of my skin. I turned with as much self-control as I could summon and smiled at the man who'd approached me.

What was a decent excuse? "I was just going to see if she wanted a coffee," I said brightly. "It looks like she's stepped out, though. I guess maybe she went to get her own."

The guy dipped his head. "Probably. I'm sure she'd have appreciated the thought, though."

I forced myself to walk onward and turned into the next stairwell, since I'd almost reached the end of the hall.

Plug in a USB drive. It'd *sounded* easy, but locating a computer where no one would see me pull off the maneuver was proving next to impossible. I wasn't some magician who could flick it in there while talking to the person at the keyboard. Although right now I really wished I was.

Mom was waiting for me at the car. I could expand my lie, make up a reason it'd taken me so long, but with every passing minute, that lie would become harder to make convincing. Maybe I should have taken Logan up on his offer to come along and create some kind of distraction, but that'd seemed so irresponsible in a hospital where lives were on the line.

That thought had barely finished passing through my head as I strode down the new hall I'd come out into when the PA system crackled to life.

"Code blue," a voice announced. "Second floor, corridor three, outside room two-seven."

The woman who'd been poised behind the nurse's station up ahead sprang into action, rushing away from the desks toward the emergency. The two other staff I could see farther down vanished into a side hallway.

The nurse's station was totally empty.

Guilt jabbed through my gut at taking advantage of someone's potentially fatal event, but I didn't have time to weigh the morality of my choice. This could be my only chance.

I darted forward and leaned over the counter toward one of the computers, fumbling for the drive at the same time. It didn't have a lid on it, thank God. Where was the port? There.

I shoved the drive into place, wiggled it to make sure it was all the way in and steady, and tugged the computer just a smidge to the side so that it was less likely anyone would notice the new accessory. I couldn't risk sticking around while the program did its work. When someone did find it, it was apparently programmed to look totally empty unless you knew how to crack its secrets. It'd be dismissed and thrown away with no one the wiser.

My pulse racing, I pushed away from the counter and spun around. I half expected a staff person to be charging toward me with an accusing yell, but there was no one around except for a nurse who was just backing out of a room several doors down. She hadn't seen anything.

I dragged in a breath and marched back to the stairwell, already formulating my excuses to Mom in my head. At the same time, I pulled out my phone from my purse, where I'd actually left it.

Everything's in place, I texted Logan. *Ready for the next phase of the plan.*

CHAPTER
SEVENTEEN

Madelyn

"Have you found anything?" I asked, glancing from the apartment's sofa over to Logan where he was perched at the kitchen island. He was in the middle of making a face at his laptop's screen. He'd been poring over the extensive collection of records he could now access from the hospital all day.

He tore his gaze from the screen to look at me with a frustrated shake of his head. "Not much. I've looked at everything from the first few months before your dad's death so far, and no unexplained illnesses or outright poisonings are coming up. But we don't know exactly when his suspicions were raised or how old *that* case was when he stumbled on it. And he might have noticed some detail that I wouldn't."

"Well, if you see anything that you think *could* be strange, let me know. I might be able to tell." I wasn't totally confident in that offer, since Dad had accumulated a lot more medical expertise than I had by that point in his life, but it'd be worth trying.

"Of course." He paused, and his attention shifted to Beckett, who was sitting at the other end of the sofa. The mafia heir had stuck around even after Slade and Dexter had needed to leave for afternoon classes, waiting to see what we might dig up. "And if Maddie can't tell, maybe that friend of yours, the toxins expert, could?"

A small smile crossed Beckett's lips. I suspected he was pleased that Logan had suggested his connections might be useful instead of snarking about them like he had so often before. "I'm sure she'd be happy to help. What about that name you mentioned from Mr. Silver's notes—the Baldwin file, I think it was?"

Logan nodded. "I already searched for that back when we first came across the mention, as well as I could at the time. But I went looking for any Baldwins again now that I have better access, and I didn't turn up any patients with that last name across all of the records that've been digitized."

My stomach knotted. "Maybe Doom's Seed or whichever of his underlings were involved realized it'd be key evidence and erased it."

Gloom crossed Logan's face. "That's definitely possible." He dipped his head and pinched the bridge of his nose with a grimace. "I'm going to keep searching, but my eyeballs feel like they're going to fall out of my head from all this staring at the screen. I think I should take a quick break."

"Don't wear yourself too thin," I said quickly, with a rush of a different kind of concern. He put too much pressure on himself as it was.

"Don't worry about me." He got up and walked to the fridge. "Anyone else want a soda?"

"I'm good," Beckett said.

I waved away the offer, my mind veering back toward the problem at hand. A rough sigh escaped me. "I wish I could do more to unravel all these threads. I hate not knowing what's really going on—now or back then. And it seems like the mystery just keeps getting bigger and more complicated."

"You've been so focused on trying to figure it out. Maybe you need a break too." Beckett scooted closer and lifted one of my socked feet onto his lap. He ran his thumbs over the arch with just the right pressure to send a tingle of released tension racing through me. "This is about your dad. I can only imagine how stressed out you are over it. But it'll be easier for you to put the pieces together if you can relax enough to give your thoughts some space."

I raised my eyebrows at him. "Are you a psychotherapist now too?"

He laughed. "I'm just speaking from personal experience, as someone who ends up in a lot of stressful conflicts."

"Hmm." I couldn't help pushing my foot into his

massaging fingers as he worked the muscles over. It did feel incredibly good. "I think I like your theory as long as this is the solution to it."

Beckett aimed a slow smile at me that sent a much more heated tingle to other parts of my body. It occurred to me abruptly that this was the first time I'd let him touch me at all intimately since I'd found out the truth about him.

I didn't want him to stop. I wanted him to touch me a whole lot more while looking at me with all that affection and desire in his gaze. My own hunger unfurled from low in my belly.

"You know," I said quietly, "I'm glad that you stuck around through everything—I'm glad that you insisted on helping. And not just because of what it means for the investigation."

Beckett paused for a second, obviously recognizing the significance of the statement. His smile widened and softened at the same time, and he reached for my other foot. "I'm glad too."

I became abruptly aware of Logan standing at the edge of my vision. He'd come around the island, standing a few feet away from the back of the sofa, studying me and Beckett. Watching Beckett's deft fingers run over my foot in a way that had my eyes rolling back and my lips clamping against a groan of approval that I didn't think would reduce the tension still in the room.

My stepbrother didn't say anything. He barely moved, standing perfectly still, his fingers clamped around the bottle of craft soda he'd grabbed without raising it to his lips.

I started to tense up again, wondering what he'd do when he snapped out of his frozen state. Would he yell at Beckett for touching me? Try to bully him out of the apartment? Or maybe snap at me for allowing the massage in the first place?

Then Logan spoke, his voice low but steady. "There are ways we could help you unwind that are a lot more effective than just a foot massage, you know."

My pulse hiccupped as his implication sank in. It obviously wasn't lost on Beckett either. The other guy's fingers paused against my foot, and he glanced over at Logan assessingly. "We?"

Logan's stance remained taut, but the corner of his mouth curled into a hint of a smirk. "If you're up for that."

"You're serious?"

I couldn't blame Beckett for feeling the need to double-check after the way Logan had responded to him before. Even after what he'd just said, it was still a shock to see my stepbrother lift his shoulders in a casual shrug. His voice stayed firm.

"It's become incredibly clear that you care about Maddie just as much as I do. And I'm not really in a position to criticize any other part of your life, considering what I've gotten myself into." Logan's gaze slid to me, both heated and tender. "I want to see Maddie happy. If that means having you on board, I can deal with it. I've been responsible for too much of her *un*happiness already."

"Logan," I said softly. "I've already forgiven you for that." And I understood why he'd done it, even if I wished he'd found a kinder approach. Wasn't I shutting out Mom and Summer the exact same way now, for the exact same reasons?

He shook his head. "It doesn't matter. The point is that you should have everything you want that you *can* have. Assuming you'd want this."

The question in those words hung in the air. A fresh tingle raced over every inch of my skin. I looked from Logan to Beckett, who was gazing back at me with his normally cool gray eyes smoldering. The last fragments of the wall I'd been holding up against my feelings for him cracked open and fell away. A swell of longing swept through me.

And how better to welcome Beckett all the way back into my life than with the man who'd once raised the most objections to his presence paving the way? We were a unified force now, no secrets or hostility left between us.

"I do," I murmured.

The instant the words left my mouth, Beckett swooped in to scoop me up in his arms. A squeal of surprise tumbled out of me as he hefted me up and around, my legs dangling.

Logan's smile grew. He motioned toward his bedroom, setting the pop bottle on a side table undrunk.

As Logan pushed open the door, Beckett carried me inside. Their scents mingled together, Beckett's crisp cologne rising from his neck and Logan's muskier smell laced throughout the room. Beckett lay me down on the bed, kneeling beside me, and Logan clambered after us to crouch at my other side.

They were a study in opposites, brown hair vs. blond, bulky brawn vs. leaner muscle. But they had so much in common, more than Logan had wanted to admit at first. And right now the most important of those things was me.

After all the arguments and the continuing power struggle between them, I wanted them both. I *needed* them both, making a precious moment with me together.

My eagerness must have shown on my face. Beckett leaned over me, his lips an inch from mine when he whispered, "Do you like the thought of being fucked by both of us, Maddie?"

A bolt of heat shot straight to my pussy. A strangled sound of agreement escaped me, and then Beckett was claiming my mouth.

But his searing kiss only lasted a moment before those damn lips made their way past the corner of my mouth. He charted a path across my cheek to my ear. His breath tickled the lobe before he nipped it between his teeth just hard enough to draw a gasp out of me.

Logan simply watched for the first minute like he had the foot massage. Then he bent down and kissed my other shoulder. His hand slid up under my shirt, his fingers teasing over my belly and tracing the base of my bra.

My nipples pebbled in anticipation. I couldn't help squirming at another delicate nip of Beckett's teeth, and Logan chuckled.

"I think our girl needs a little more attention," he said.

Beckett eased back as if instinctively understanding him, and they both reached for the hem of my shirt together. I sat up a little and raised my arms so they could peel it off, and Beckett took the opportunity to unhook my bra as well.

"Good thinking," Logan said with warm amusement, and tugged the garment right off me.

Beckett matched his tone. "We can't let any part of her be neglected."

He rolled his thumb over my nipple, and Logan dipped his head to suck the other into his mouth. My back arched at the dual jolts of pleasure, a whimper I couldn't restrain leaving my lips.

Beckett went back to kissing my jaw and the side of my neck as he teased the peak of my breast to a harder nub. Logan applied his tongue and teeth as well as his lips, every swipe and graze making me tremble harder. My panties were soaked now. My nerves quivered with increasing bliss.

"You smell so good," Beckett muttered into my hair.

Logan raised his head and grinned, a spark lighting in his eyes. "I know where she'll smell even more delicious."

His fingers hooked around the waist of my jeans, one hand moving to quickly flick open the fly. My heart thumping faster, I lifted my hips to let him tug them off me. But then I couldn't help eyeing their shirts and pants while I lay there almost completely exposed between them. "I shouldn't be the only one getting naked around here."

Beckett arched an eyebrow at Logan. "I guess she does have a point."

They both reached for their shirts, Beckett needing to unbutton his partway down, Logan simply peeling off his fitted tee. As my stepbrother slid his jeans down his thighs, I couldn't stop my gaze from roaming over the sculpted body I'd never seen on full display before.

He had his Vigil tattoo, a hawk that matched the ones I'd seen on both Slade and Dexter, imprinted on his right hip. Several inches higher, a pale scar across his abdomen reminded me of the surgery that had saved his life and given him his second chance all those years ago.

I yanked my gaze farther up, knowing how little Logan liked to think about or be reminded about his transplant. But he didn't appear concerned right now. He was toying with the waist of my panties. As my eyes met his, he yanked them down after my pants.

He trailed his hand back up my inner thigh and circled his fingers around the spot where I was aching most. I swayed toward him, and he traced his thumb right down my seam.

At my moan, his pleased laugh carried through the room. "Good girl."

He thrust a finger right inside me while pressing his thumb down on my clit. As I rocked into his touch, Beckett focused his attention on my chest, palming one breast and slicking his tongue over the peak of the other.

Bliss radiated through every part of my body. Beckett sucked on my nipple at the same moment as Logan plunged a second finger into me, and I cried out. Need condensed low in my belly, a burning ache for release.

Logan pumped his fingers faster, but he seemed to have decided he wouldn't be satisfied with propelling me over the edge that way. He pulled farther to the side with a few more strokes and glanced at Beckett.

"Why don't you bring her the rest of the way there? Take her from behind. She deserves it good and deep."

Beckett held his gaze for a moment, a silent understanding appearing to form between them. Logan was proving just how far he'd go to accept Beckett into every part of my life. A lump filled my throat even as hunger seared through my veins.

As Beckett reached me, I flipped myself over. He pressed kisses down my spine, his hand caressing my ass. I pressed into his touch, but my attention settled on Logan's cock jutting rigidly from between his thighs. My mouth watered.

"This isn't supposed to be only about me," I said, shooting him a wicked smile, and leaned over to lap my tongue around his shaft.

The noise that left him made the gesture so worth it.

I wrapped my mouth right around his erection as foil ripped behind me.

Beckett delved his hand between my legs and sucked in a breath at my wetness. "You're good with this, Maddie?" he said, one final acknowledgment of the fissure that'd opened between us.

I never wanted us to be at odds like that again. I hummed encouragingly, and he pressed one more kiss to my back before rubbing his cock over my slit. Then he pushed right in.

There was nothing quite like the sensation of taking two men into me at the same time. Logan was rocking into my mouth, his breath coming short, and Beckett groaned as he sank all the way into my pussy. My channel stretched to encompass him with a heady rush of pleasure.

"Tug on her hair," Beckett suggested in a rough voice.

Logan grunted and wound his fingers through several strands. He applied pressure at a rhythm that matched the bobbing of my mouth and Beckett's quickening strokes inside me. Little sparks of sensation lit up across my scalp, only heightening the bliss of the moment.

"Fuck her hard," Logan said to Beckett, his voice breaking over a few of the words. "That's how she likes it."

To my immense delight, Beckett didn't hesitate to obey. He thrust deeper and faster at the same time, filling me so well that I panted around Logan's erection before sucking harder in turn. The wave of pleasure rising inside me surged higher with each stroke.

Beckett leaned over my back and tucked his hand around me to finger my clit. My moan reverberated over Logan's cock, and his hips jerked.

"I'm going to come," he rasped, tensing as if to pull back, but I clutched his thigh to hold him in place. With a groan, he spilled himself into my mouth. I swallowed until every drop of his salty release had coursed down my throat.

Beckett pounded into me harder still, and my lips popped from around Logan's cock with a cry. More gasps spilled out of me as he plunged into me again and again, circling my clit at the same time, sending me spiraling so high—

I exploded with a shudder, my channel clamping around his shaft. My face dropped into the bedspread as I keened my release. Beckett swore under his breath and followed me with one final thrust.

He slumped over me with a happy sigh and then rolled us onto our sides so I faced Logan. My stepbrother sprawled out next to me and slipped his arm around my waist, not appearing to care if he brushed against the other man.

A different sort of joy bloomed in my chest and spread through every limb. We'd come so far to make it to this moment where these two men could accept each other and shower me with affection side by side, and no one could take that away from us.

CHAPTER EIGHTEEN

Slade

Striding out of the campus gym, I was dogged by an ache in my chest that wouldn't fade. I'd pushed myself hard enough in my workout that I'd needed to sit in the locker room for ten minutes recovering before I could confidently make it in and out of the showers with my prosthetic off, but despite wearing myself ragged, I hadn't managed to burn away as much of my emotions as I'd hoped.

The urge to go dancing itched at me. I hadn't hit the clubs in weeks, and I missed letting loose to the beats in an anonymous mass of people.

But it wasn't just me and a bunch of strangers on my favorite dance floor anymore. It was me, the dance floor, and Beckett. Knowing he owned the club, I couldn't see it the same way. It was his place, not mine. But at the same time, some part of me balked at the idea of being forced to go someplace else.

Heading along the paths across campus, I managed to keep my strides steady even though my muscles were wobbly from the workout. My gaze automatically scanned the other people passing by for anyone who looked suspicious, but how would I know anyway?

A painfully familiar voice called out from behind me. "Slade! Wait up."

I turned to see Maddie jogging over across the lawn, her backpack dangling from one shoulder. With her pale hair windblown and a flush of exertion turning her cheeks rosy, she was an even prettier sight than usual.

My spirits should have lifted, but instead they sank. A sense of wariness swept over me, more to do with myself than her.

She was one more reminder of all the ways I'd fallen short.

I couldn't take my frustration out on her, though. I plastered a smile onto my face and fell into step with her when she caught up with me. Her open smile in return sent a jab of guilt through my stomach.

"What have you been up to?" she asked, tucking her hand around my elbow as easy as anything.

God, I wanted her. Why did this have to be so hard?

I summoned my usual breezy tone. "Oh, you know, classes, working out, the usual."

"Off to anyplace interesting now?"

"I figured I'd grab dinner at the pub by the fine arts

building. You know those creative types, they've got good taste in food too."

She laughed and squeezed my arm. "Would you like some company? I barely even had lunch—I could definitely go for a good burger."

Hell, I wanted her around me every moment of every day. But I had to be realistic. And there was no point in indulging my whims right now—I was in too shitty a mood for her to miss it if she spent much more time with me. If she hadn't *already* picked up on it.

I groped for an excuse. "I actually have some reading for one of my classes that I need to get done while I'm eating. But I'll see you back at the apartment later."

Maddie slowed, pulling me to a stop with her. My heart plummeted even farther as I took in her expression, her eyes clouded, her forehead furrowing. She studied me through several uncomfortable thumps of my heart.

"Are you avoiding me?" she said finally, her voice rough. "It's been feeling kind of like you've been pulling back from the other guys and from me lately. Is something wrong?"

I forced a chuckle and made a dismissive wave of my hand. "Of course not. I do have to get serious about my schoolwork every now and then to make sure they don't kick me out of this place. I love having you with me, but I won't be able to concentrate with those lips so close, Piccolina."

I reached out and brushed my finger over her mouth, provoking a twitch of a smile.

"I can see how hard you're *trying* to be convincing, Slade," she said.

Fuck. "Convincing? I'm just speaking the truth."

She grasped my hand and tugged me away from the path, over to the shelter of a tree where we were away from the students passing by. Her gaze stayed fixed on my face. "Tell me what's going on."

I couldn't. I couldn't explain it all to her. Not until I could come to terms with my feelings myself. "It's really nothing," I told her. "Nothing worth talking about."

"You know, you never have to talk to me if you don't want to. I'm not going to force you to stick around, but I don't want you to pretend either. You should never feel like you need to fake anything with me."

Her words cracked something within me. Faking. That was all I'd been doing since starting the Vigil with the guys. Since the moment we began calling ourselves the Vigilante Kings, I'd been pretending. I was a total imposter in the job that I'd been doing for all these years.

"What's the point in sticking around?" I asked, shaking my head. "I want to be there for you and the guys, sure. But I used to feel like I actually contributed, and now that Beckett's in the mix, it's obvious that I'm just there on the sidelines. I was always the least useful one even when it was just the three of us. So, I'm dead weight. And that's fine. But why should you bother sticking around with *me* when you've got three other great guys?"

Maddie stared at me, confusion etched across her face. "Do you really feel that way?"

My head drooped. "I wasn't planning on telling you. I don't want to get *you* down about it. It is what it is."

"Hey." She grasped my hand tighter until I looked up and met her eyes. "Let's start with the most important thing. You're not dead weight. Not to me, not to the Vigil. Not to anybody. I don't think any of us could function properly without you, Slade."

When I made a scoffing sound, she frowned. "Is it the sharing that's bothering you? Is it too much—and you're trying to let me down easy or something?"

I sputtered for a second before I found my words. "Maddie, the last thing I'd want is to let go of you. All I *think* about is you, and that's the problem. It's going to be so hard if you leave, so it's easier if I put the distance there first."

The furrow in her forehead deepened. "Why would you think that it's better to assume things won't work out? What if I *don't* leave? Are you so sure that I will?"

I made a vague gesture with my hand, the ache expanding through my chest so intensely it was suffocating. "It just… doesn't make sense for you to stay."

Maddie let out a huff. "You just talked about how much you want me. Why can't you believe that I'd want you just as much—just as much as the other guys? You make me laugh; you taught me how to dance. You compliment me in a million different languages. You're there for the people you care about no matter what. Why *wouldn't* I want to be with you?"

A prickling sensation rose up through my gut. I knew the answer to that question instinctively, but I didn't want to say it. I didn't talk about that shit with anyone. It shouldn't affect anyone but me.

I was supposed to be the one making her laugh and tossing compliments at her, not the one dragging her down with the crap I kept buried deep inside.

"Slade," she said softly, searching my gaze. "Please talk to me. I want to understand where this is coming from."

My throat constricted. How could I deny her when she was practically begging me? It would be worse to leave her wondering, thinking maybe she'd done something wrong, wouldn't it?

My voice came out uncomfortably gruff. "My own *mother* thought I was too defective to be around. She couldn't stand to keep taking care of me—she left my dad, the love of her life, because of it."

Maddie's eyes widened. "You don't really think that's why, do you?"

"People don't stay," I said with a rasp. "I can entertain them and make them happy for a little while now because I work my ass off at it, but in the end… if even the person who's *most* supposed to be there can't be bothered…"

"Slade." Maddie wrapped me in a hug so sudden I stiffened up before I registered what she was doing. My arms came around her of their own accord, my eyes burning as I tipped my head next to hers. The sweet smell of her hair filled my nose.

"No offense," she murmured, her breath tickling my neck warmly, "but your mom was a total jerk. No one deserves to be abandoned by a parent. But she probably left for reasons that had nothing to do with your leg. And if your birth defect *did* have anything to do with it, then she's an even bigger jerk."

A strangled sort of laugh tumbled out of me. "I'd pay good money to find her just so I could watch you tell her off like that."

Maddie hummed dismissively and squeezed me tighter. "She's not important anymore. She made her choices, jerky as they were, and now she's gone. You're here, and you're amazing. I love you exactly the way you are. I love your sense of humor and how much energy you always bring to every conversation, I love the fact that you don't let your leg slow you down and even manage to turn it into something fun with your crazy stories."

As my mind whirled with her declaration, she pulled back just far enough to hold my gaze again. "I love *you*, Slade. Everything you are."

It was impossible not to believe her when she said the words so emphatically, her blue eyes piercing into mine as if they were going to claim my soul. I'd have let her if I could offer it up.

I blinked hard, grappling with the wave of emotion that was rushing through me, a lot more of it good than it'd been before but still a mess. My voice came out choked. "I love you too."

I tugged her back to me, winding my fingers in her soft hair, and pressed my mouth to hers as if I could brand the truth of that statement into her. She kissed me back just as hard. The impact of what we'd just said reverberated through me, and all my despondency fell away in its wake. Maddie's touch and the memory of her words ringing through my head banished the gnawing doubts.

She saw someone amazing in me, and I was going to be that amazing guy with every particle of my being.

When we finally eased apart, our breaths a little ragged, Maddie grinned at me. At the sparkle in her blue eyes, I found my usual optimism came to me without any hesitation at all.

I tweaked one of her blond locks and grinned right back at her. "What do you say we go and get that dinner we both need?"

CHAPTER
NINETEEN

Madelyn

I leaned back in my chair and massaged my temples, restraining a groan. I'd been stuffing facts about genetics into my head for the past few hours in preparation for next week's exam, and my brain felt ready to explode.

Before I could really consider taking a break, though, my ringtone pealed from my purse. I dug it out. At the sight of Beckett's name on the screen, I yanked it to my ear.

"Hey," I said. "What's up?"

"Hey, Maddie. I just wanted to give you a heads up that I've got some things I'd like to send your way."

"What kind of things?"

He paused. "Is everything all right? You sound exhausted."

I let out a grunt of frustration. "Just studying woes. I could use a change of pace."

"Well, I can certainly give you that." He chuckled, but it sounded a bit strained. "My people have dug up a bunch of files related to both the warehouse and the seafood market. I haven't spotted anything useful in them, but I thought it'd be good to have you give them a glance too since you'd have a better idea how anything might connect to your dad."

I sat up a little straighter. "Of course. I'll go through them right away."

"Thanks, Maddie. I know if there's anything in there, you'll find it."

His voice had gone distant, as if his mind had already moved on to other considerations. I frowned. "Is everything okay with *you*? You seem kind of distracted."

Beckett paused again and then allowed himself a deep sigh. "It's nothing to do with the case or your dad —nothing for you to worry about. I've just had an issue within the family business come up out of left field. It appears that rumors have been going around that I've been off my game lately, not focused on the work or committed to overseeing our people."

I couldn't hold back a scoffing noise. "They have to know that's not really true."

"I'm not sure. A few of my employees have abandoned ship. Others might be on the fence. I'm about to address a bunch of my direct reports at a meeting to hopefully put an end to the unrest."

Why would the people under him believe he was anything less than the totally dedicated man I'd always observed him to be? "I just don't understand—" I started, and then the answer clicked in my head.

My throat tightened. "Oh. It's because of me, isn't it? All the stuff to do with the investigation and protecting me."

Beckett's voice firmed. "Maddie—there've definitely been some questions about some of the tasks I've set people on, but it isn't your fault. They need to trust me to handle my personal concerns and aspects of our business that they're not privy to at my discretion. I'm going to set them straight."

My stomach twisted. I didn't love what Beckett did for a living, but I knew how much it meant to him— and how important it was in the grand scheme of things that he *kept* doing it rather than someone else pushing their way into his spot. If he lost his standing with his underlings because he'd tried to help me…

"What if I came and helped you set them straight?" I blurted out before I could rethink the impulse.

"What?" Beckett said with obvious surprise.

"Let me come with you. If they already know you're dating someone, they might as well see who I am and hear right from my mouth what the real situation is."

He hesitated. "I don't know if that's the best idea."

"Why? You don't think they'd outright *attack* me if I'm there with you, do you?"

A chill shivered over my skin, but Beckett immediately answered. "No, definitely not. They aren't animals. But you know what kind of work I'm involved in. They aren't your typical office workers either—not most of them, anyway. They might make some harsh comments. They won't necessarily be polite."

A nervous laugh tumbled out of me. "I think I can handle some rudeness. It'll be a step up from psycho murderers threatening my family. Anyway, I'd like to see you at work. It'll help me totally come to terms with who you are and why."

Maybe it was the last part that convinced him. "All right. If you insist. Can you get to the coffee shop just past the north entrance to the university in fifteen minutes? I'll pick you up around back on my way over to the meeting."

I stood up, already reaching for my purse. "No problem at all."

I hustled down the stairs and out into the warm spring air. The lingering winter chill had completely faded, and I was starting to taste hints of summer on the breeze. I might have enjoyed it if my heart hadn't been thumping in anticipation of the meeting I was about to attend. What had I gotten myself into?

Beckett would be right beside me the whole time. He wouldn't have agreed to let me join him if he'd thought I'd be in any actual danger.

I'd only partly reassured myself when my phone rang again. I pulled it out of my purse as I hurried around the fitness center and saw it was Summer calling this time.

My first instinct was to ignore the call and avoid another awkward conversation with her. But the idea of treating my bestie that way made me wince inwardly.

I forced myself to answer. "Hey, Summer! How's it going?"

"Not great, Madds," Summer retorted in a dry tone that wasn't as spirited as usual. "My best friend's been icing me out of her life."

I winced outwardly that time. "I swear it isn't like that—"

"But it is, Maddie. I'm tired of the excuses and the vague explanations. You're obviously hiding something from me, something bad. I want you to tell me what's going on. We've always been honest with each other. You know you can count on me, no matter what's wrong. Don't shut me out."

My stomach knotted up. I didn't know what to say to her. "I'm telling you as much as I can," I said apologetically. "You have to believe me that it's better if you don't know more about what's going on right now. *I* don't even know exactly what's wrong."

Summer snorted. "Bullshit. You know a hell of a lot more than you've been telling me."

"I'm still sorting it all out."

"Then sort it out with *me*," Summer pleaded, so emphatically that tears pricked at my eyes. "I don't care how big or how stupid it is. I just need to know that you're okay—or that I'm helping you if you're not. Please."

Summer wasn't normally one to beg. My throat ached with the urge to spill the details about our investigation after all. But an image of Mom right after the car accident flashed through my mind—her body all bruised and broken in the hospital bed. Nausea swept through me.

"I'm sorry," I choked out. "I'll tell you everything when I can—I promised you that, and I mean it. But I've got to go now. I really am sorry."

I hung up without giving her a chance to argue more and turned off the phone. Guilt sat like a boulder in my gut, but there was nothing I could do about it. I'd have felt ten times as guilty if I'd dragged her into this mess and she got hurt.

Within a minute of my ambling behind the coffee shop, Beckett's familiar sedan pulled up. I hopped inside as quickly as possible and buckled my seatbelt as he took off again. When I glanced over at him, he shot me a smile, but it was tight, and his eyes were dark with obvious worry.

"You've never had anything like this happen before, have you?" I said. "Your people doubting you?"

How could he have when I found it so hard to imagine anyone doubting him even in the current situation. He'd always seemed like an impervious force.

Beckett shrugged. "The kind of career I have isn't meant to be easy or conflict-free. I'll deal with it. I just want you in the crossfire as little as possible."

I set my hand on his arm. "Hey. You've pulled out all the stops to protect me. I want to be able to do the same for you in whatever small ways I can. If we're together, then it isn't going to be one-sided."

The smile he aimed at me then was softer around the edges. "Duly noted. And thank you."

When he pulled up to the curb, I realized he was parking off to the side of the office building where we'd had our brief picnic lunch the other day, the one where he was setting up his pro bono clinic. He came around the side of the car as I got out and tucked his hand around my elbow. "Stay with me, all right?"

"Nowhere else I'd want to be."

We strode to the building together and ducked in through a side door. Beckett led me down a hall toward an open doorway. Muttering voices carried from inside.

We stepped into a room that must have been one of the unclaimed office spaces, empty of furniture and cubicles, just open space with a high ceiling. But that space was crowded with people.

There had to be at least fifty of them milling around the room. Several were dressed similarly to Beckett's usual business casual style in slacks and button-up shirts, as if they might work in this office once it was set up. The others, though, clearly came from other lines of work. I spotted multiple tattoos and glints of nose, lip, and eyebrow piercings, along with a rainbow of different hair colors, many clearly dyed. Leather jackets, faded tees, and scuffed jeans were more typical fashion choices for that part of the crowd.

It wasn't as if I'd never seen people with vivid hair dye and interesting piercings before. Hell, there were students like that in all of my college classes. But the less professional-looking employees who'd turned up for this meeting radiated the sort of menace that I'd never felt from any of my peers. Their postures and expressions gave off an aura of toughness and hostility.

My muscles tensed instinctively with apprehension. But next to me, Beckett had composed his face into calm confidence. He circumnavigated the crowd with me at his side like a king ready to address his subjects. There was no denying he was a natural leader.

I took his lead and kept my head high. I wouldn't let my nervousness show. I trusted him to keep me safe, and I had to prove that to them, or I couldn't ask *them* to trust him to look after them too.

Skeptical gazes raked over my body. Someone let out a mocking whistle, and a couple of cat calls echoed off the high ceiling. Beckett ignored them, so I did as well.

All that mattered was that these people were the ones Beckett could normally count on. They *wanted* to stand with him, to believe in him, just like I did. Which meant we had one important thing in common no matter how many other divides lay between us.

There was a small, raised platform at the far end of the room, about half a foot off the ground. Beckett stepped onto it and guided me up with him. Then he turned to face his people.

It said something about how much respect they still

had for him that the muttering trailed off within a few seconds of him casting his gaze over the crowd. Everyone from the office workers to the toughs fixed their gazes on him and waited in silence to hear what he'd say first.

"Thank you for coming to speak with me today," Beckett said in a steady, assured voice. "I know there've been rumors buzzing around about my conduct recently, and I felt it was important to set the record straight and answer any questions you might have. First off, I can assure you that I'm fully on top of all things related to our business. My focus hasn't faltered, and I'm sure if you think about it, you won't be able to find any instances where important matters were neglected."

A hesitant murmur rippled through the crowd, sounding more like agreement than argument. That was a good start. My spirits started to lift.

"I *have* made some new social connections," Beckett went on, touching my elbow again. "But they haven't interfered with my ability to oversee everything we're working toward, and I hope none of you would fault me for having a life."

The corner of his lips quirked upward, a wry note entering his voice, and several people throughout the room chuckled. But others narrowed their eyes at me.

"Just how much time *are* you spending on your side-piece slut instead of on keeping things running smoothly?" someone demanded from the back of the crowd.

My nerves twitched, but I held myself still. Beside

me, Beckett's expression tightened. I could tell from the flash in his eyes that he was about to speak in my defense, probably with anger, and I doubted that would reassure the people here who needed it most.

As much as I appreciated his protectiveness, I jumped in before he could speak. "Since you've obviously been misinformed, let me give you a few facts. Beckett and I have only gone on a few dates in the past month, and that's the only time he's dedicated to me. Even in the short times he has been able to spend with me, I know his business has never been far from his mind. He's cut dates short because he had meetings and other concerns to take care of."

My heart was racing now. A droplet of sweat rolled down my neck under my hair as I took in the skeptical gazes evaluating me. But I met those gazes without flinching.

I'd gone up against gangsters and thugs before. I wasn't going to let these people intimidate me.

"That's not all we've been hearing about," someone else hollered from the crowd. "Nice try, little girl."

I glowered in their general direction. "Any time Beckett has spent on matters other than business recently has been to tackle someone who's been threatening both me and the business you seem so concerned about him taking care of. He's working to protect all of your interests and his own as well as mine."

"For now," a woman grumbled.

I cut my gaze in her direction, my pulse still wobbly

but my stance increasingly steady. "Frankly, I've never met anyone more committed to his work than the man beside me, and I wouldn't want him to slack off on it. You don't have to worry about me distracting him. And if you don't already know that he gives this business and the people working with him his all, then I don't think *you've* been paying enough attention."

Someone made a noise of protest, but Beckett intervened before they got any further than that. His hands were clenched but loosely, and his eyes shone for a moment as he looked at me. Then he turned to his employees.

"As you should be able to see, I have nothing to hide. The real distraction here are these rumors, which are purposefully designed to unsettle you. They're absolutely untrue. Someone is trying to undermine my leadership. But you know me and what I stand for. I've never let you down, and I don't intend to start."

A more animated murmur followed that declaration. The idea that their leader might be under attack seemed to rile up his underlings even though some had moments ago been criticizing him.

Beckett went on, motioning to the crowd. "We're all dedicated to keeping this empire working as it should. You can count on me, and I'd better be able to count on you. Go and find out who's stirring up trouble against the Storm, and let's deal with them together."

Voices rose in approval while several of the underlings ducked their heads with shamed grimaces. At Beckett's wave, they all hustled toward the door as if eager to prove themselves to their leader. Relief trickled through my chest, but a deeper tension stopped it from filling me.

I turned to Beckett as the last of his people slipped past the doorway. "Do you really think someone's still out to displace you? That someone from the outside started the rumors on purpose? I thought Doom's Seed and his lieutenant were backing off."

Beckett swiped his hand across his mouth. His shoulders had relaxed a little with the end of the meeting, but at my question, he only looked weary.

"That's what Doom's Seed promised, but I'm becoming increasingly sure he was lying. This has to be Lindell sowing doubts about me, and he couldn't do it now without his boss knowing about it."

"Why?" I had to ask.

Beckett was silent for a long moment. "There's only one logical reason I can think of. Doom's Seed is planning on making a grab for the Storm's territory here. For *my* territory. And soon."

CHAPTER
TWENTY

Madelyn

My eyes were starting to glaze over. I dragged them away from my laptop's screen, rubbed them, and gazed blearily across the main campus library where I'd been sitting for the past couple of hours. Beckett had sent me a lot of files yesterday, but so far nothing I'd seen in them seemed at all connected to my dad.

I wasn't alone in my search. Logan, Slade, and Dexter were all sitting amid the rows of computers at the other end of the first floor, searching the digitized database of old newspaper and magazine articles with local news that might give us some clue about whichever of Doom's Seed's illegal businesses Dad had gotten wrapped up in.

So far they hadn't turned up anything either, as far as I knew. Logan had been leaving his computer periodically and coming around to see how I was doing, as if I were straining anything other than my eyes sitting here in this upholstered chair. But there'd been something so intense in his eyes and his voice that I hadn't hassled him about his concern, just reassured him. Each time, he'd lingered for several more seconds before seeming to tear himself away.

So it wasn't a surprise to see him ambling over again now. He nodded toward my computer. "Still nothing?"

"Yeah," I said, and restrained a yawn. It wasn't even noon yet, but I hadn't been sleeping all that well these days. "I don't think I can stand to stare at this screen any more. Maybe I'll take a little walk around." I shut my laptop.

Logan's attention homed in on me again, so penetrating it made my skin tingle. "I could use that too. Come with me?" He extended his hand.

Why not? I tucked my computer under my arm and let him tug me out of my chair. "Where are we going?"

"Not far."

He kept his hand around mine and led me along the wall to one of the study rooms that lined it. This door didn't have a reserved sign on it.

Logan opened it with an air of purpose, escorted me inside, and switched the sign over to reserved. As the door thumped shut, he clicked over the lock, lifted the laptop from me to toss it onto the meeting table behind him, and pushed me up against the door.

His hands fell to my hips, pinning me in place. His gaze pinned me too, staring down at me as if he were memorizing my face, in awe of every angle. A heady tingle raced down my back at his passionate examination, his musky scent winding around me with his closeness.

"What are you doing?" I asked, my voice coming out breathless.

He bent so his forehead rested against mine. "I can't get enough of you, you know. The curve of your lips." He brushed a finger across them, provoking more tingles. "Your cute little nose." He tapped it. "This hair. It's so soft. And the way you react when I play with it…"

He twirled a few strands around his fingers and gave them a light tug. I couldn't stop my eyelids from fluttering at the sparks that shot through my scalp. Heat was pooling between my thighs.

Logan drew my head back farther, exposing my neck. He dropped his head and pressed a trail of kisses along my throat. I quivered against him, a gasp tumbling out of me.

"I was thinking," he muttered, pulling his lips away as if it was an effort to do so. He left his hand in my hair, but he released the tension there, allowing me to look up at him. "It hasn't been just the two of us since we cleared the air. Since that night two years ago, I haven't been with you the way I wanted to, and even then…"

He paused, shaking his head, regret etched in his

features. "It wasn't how I wanted it to go. Not our first time. Not *any* time."

"I know," I said, an ache forming in my chest. I believed him, now more than ever.

He stroked his fingers over my hair, meeting my eyes again. "I don't mind that you're with the other guys too. I've made my peace with that—and honestly it's fucking *hot* watching how good we can make you feel when we're working together. But I want a little bit of you all to myself."

"Of course," I said quietly, curling my fingers into the front of his shirt. "You've got me. There'll always be pieces that are special to just the two of us."

"I want this too. I want what our first time should have been. Things are getting so dangerous, and I don't want to wait any longer. I love you. And it's not going to feel right until I've written over all that crap from the past."

My heart swelled at his admission. He loved me. Logan Brooks *loved* me.

Before the answering words that'd been true for longer than I could say spilled from my mouth, he claimed my lips again. His tongue flicked along my bottom lip, making me whimper. He molded his body against mine, pressing me into the door with his massive muscular frame.

The feel of him set me on fire. My nipples pebbled inside my bra without any further contact. I was pretty sure my panties had liquified. I kissed him back with everything I had in me, wrapping my arms around his shoulders and tugging him closer still.

Logan kissed me again and again until my lips felt swollen. He nipped them and moved to my jaw. I ran my fingers over his short-cropped hair, and he groaned.

"I always thought you were amazing," he murmured against my skin. "Seeing you stand up for people the way you did in high school, how you never let anyone intimidate you." He shook his head in bemusement, his mouth grazing my neck. "It was so fucking hard staying just friendly after my dad and your mom started dating. I didn't want to make things awkward, but you were right there, all the time, beautiful and bold and smart. I thought I was going to go crazy keeping my hands off of you."

I shivered in his embrace with the thrill his words sent through me. I couldn't hold back my own confession. "I started falling for you all the way back in junior high." My voice hitched when he nipped the crook of my shoulder. "*You* were always so cool and confident—you stood up for me back then, remember? But you always seemed out of reach."

Logan let out a scoffing sound, pulling back to meet my eyes. "Me, better than you? No fucking way. If anything, you're out of *my* league."

The corners of my mouth twitched. "Maybe we can just agree that we're very happy we finally made it to this moment."

"Hell, yes."

Without warning, Logan lifted me up and spun me

toward the narrow couch along the study room's side wall. He laid me down on the cushions and braced himself over me with his hips resting against mine. The bulge between his thighs aligned with my core, and with just the slightest squirm I was pretty sure I'd be the one going crazy soon.

There was no denying where we were headed. I wanted to say one thing before I got totally swept up in the collision of our bodies.

I reached up and trailed my fingers down the side of Logan's face, gazing up into his eyes. "I love you too. So much. That's why I couldn't give up on you."

His mouth tightened. "I wish you hadn't needed to consider giving up, but I'm so fucking grateful you keep believing in me, Maddie."

I smiled. "Totally worth it."

Then I dragged him down to me, bringing our bodies flush together and pressing my lips against his. He met me without hesitation. His mouth parted against mine, a flick of his tongue setting my lips tingling again. I could only close my eyes and hang on for the ride.

Logan pulled away to lift my shirt up over my bra, exposing my breasts. He eased down the cups and rolled his thumb over one nipple before sucking it into his mouth. I swallowed a moan, distantly aware of the library activity on the other side of this room's door.

His other hand slid between us to the aching spot between my legs. He yanked open the fly of my jeans and tucked his fingers right inside my panties. When the tips brushed over my clit, I gasped at the jolt of bliss.

"How do you want me to fuck you, Maddie?" he murmured, stroking me as I started to rock into his touch.

"I don't care," I whispered. "I just want you."

"Fuck. I'm going to make you feel so good. Like no other time could possibly matter. You won't be able to remember anything but this."

My breath shuddered out of me, and then he was yanking my jeans and panties right off. Voices filtered through the wall from the library, and I bit my lip to try to hold back another moan.

Libraries were really not the best place for this kind of encounter, and yet knowing how close we were to being caught somehow made it twice as hot. As I'd found out with Slade to impressive effect weeks ago.

Logan tugged his jeans and boxers down too. His cock sprang free, thick and corded, so hard I ached even more just looking at it.

But he wasn't rushing things. He cupped his hand around my cunt again and dipped a finger right inside me.

"I'm going to take you so high," he promised, pulsing his hand as he added a second finger. I gasped as he swiveled them in a motion that had me bucking into his hand. "That's right. Ride my fingers, baby."

He fucked me with his hand until I was teetering on the edge, waves of pleasure washing over me. My teeth were digging a hole in my lip from holding back my eager noises. When one whimper slipped out anyway, Logan's breath hitched.

"I want to bury myself so deep inside of you that you won't forget this for years to come. God, I'm never letting you go."

He pumped his fingers inside me a few more times and then grabbed a condom from his pocket. What felt like an instant later, he'd rolled it over himself and was plunging into me.

He filled me so well I couldn't restrain my next moan. Logan clamped his mouth down over mine, swallowing the sound with a kiss.

Our bodies smacked together, both of us moving frantically as if we couldn't get close enough. Logan met my eyes, holding my gaze even as his hazed with pleasure. "Love you," he murmured again. "So fucking much."

"I love you too," I whispered back.

I gripped his shoulder and hugged him to me. He returned the embrace even though it momentarily slowed his thrusts. Then he adjusted our position, lifting my ass off the sofa, and drove into me even deeper than before.

A thready cry burst from my lips. I clamped them shut and clutched him tightly. He pounded into me again and again and then I was bursting apart with a white-hot blaze that really did feel as if it was searing away all the pain that had ever existed between us.

Logan groaned softly at the same time. His hips

jerked as he followed me over the edge, both of us crashing into the final surge of ecstasy together.

Logan sagged over me but didn't let too much of his weight bear down. He pressed a kiss to my temple and then looked at me with so much tenderness my pulse stuttered.

"I'm never pushing you away again," he said like a vow. "Acting like a prick didn't keep you out of danger anyway, so I can admit it was an idiotic move."

"You were trying to scare me away from the danger, but I don't scare easily," I said with a breathless laugh, and halted. Several thoughts collided in my head with that statement, setting off a spark of inspiration.

I nudged Logan off me so I could sit up and grab my jeans. "I need my computer. I think I might have figured it out."

Logan raised his eyes with a chuckle. "I didn't expect the experience to be *quite* that enlightening."

I swatted his arm. "I'm serious. You want me out of danger—let's get this figured out."

"Not going to argue with you there."

He did insist on stealing one more kiss before snatching my laptop off the table where he'd left it. I flipped it open and hastily clicked through to a set of photographs Beckett had sent me from the seafood market.

Logan sat next to me on the sofa, peering at the screen alongside me. "What are we looking for?"

I flicked through several photos before my heart

leapt. I stopped and jabbed my finger at the screen. "Those."

The photo showed one of the storerooms where the market received deliveries. It was stacked with coolers, a few of which were marked with the word WARNING and a picture of a spiny-looking fish.

"What about them?" Logan asked. "Those would be for the rare fish that are poisonous or something, right? I think there are some that are legal. And any that aren't, they wouldn't be advertising it."

"Exactly," I said. "You'd assume they're for transporting toxic fish for restaurants and other special buyers. And no one would want to open those boxes unless they have permission because they wouldn't want to mess with something dangerous and risk getting hurt."

Logan's eyes widened. "I think I see where you're going with this."

"I need to tell Beckett so he can check it out right away. We don't know how much evidence they've already gotten rid of."

I dug my phone out of my purse and dialed the number as fast as I could. Beckett picked up on the second ring. "Maddie. Is everything okay?"

"I think it might be *good*, actually," I said. "I think I might have figured out a key part of the scheme."

His voice perked up immediately. "Seriously? Give me all the details."

I studied the photograph as I spoke. "The seafood market does at least a little business in poisonous fish.

They're transported in containers that warn people away from messing with them."

"Oh, I already looked into that. The market has a license for things like lionfish and stonefish. There's nothing illegal about that aspect, and they wouldn't need to smuggle or hide them. From what Anthea said, your dad's symptoms don't look like any fish toxin anyway."

"That's not what I'm thinking," I said. "What if it's not always fish in those containers? What if Doom's Seed's people are moving their illegal merchandise in those specific coolers, knowing that no one who isn't approved will risk opening them and digging around inside? No one wants to get hurt."

Beckett sucked in a breath. "You're right. That would be a perfect disguise."

"We need to figure out all the places the market was shipping those supposed poisonous fish to. If any of those places isn't somewhere that should be dealing in actual fish, we've got a lead."

"This could be everything we need." He let out an exhilarated laugh. "Good job, Maddie. Hold on." His voice became muffled briefly as he passed on instructions, I assumed to computer-savvy employees he was working with right now. What had he been busy with when I'd called?

Beckett's voice became clearer again. "I've got some other things to handle, but I'll talk to you again as soon as we have— Shit."

At the dark tone of his last word, my body tensed up. "What's wrong?"

Beckett barked a couple of muffled instructions before answering me, sounding abruptly harried. "I was afraid of this. It looks like Doom's Seed or his lieutenant are making a more aggressive move on my territory— right now. I've got to go. You and the guys keep an eye out for trouble and be careful."

"Of course," I said, my throat constricting. Before I could ask if there was any way I could help, the line had already gone dead.

My gaze shot to Logan. "Doom's Seed is attacking Beckett's people. He's worried about us. Maybe we should go back to the apartment rather than staying here?" That smaller space with only one door and windows too high to easily reach felt much more secure than the wide-open library.

Logan frowned at my statement and jerked his head in a nod. We sprang to our feet and rushed out of the study room.

"I'll meet you guys by the front doors," I said to Logan, and he loped over to alert Slade and Dexter.

I shoved my computer into my backpack and hefted that over my shoulders, adjusting my purse as I did. My feet carried me across the carpeted floor as fast as I dared to walk without risking getting yelled at by one of the librarians.

I was just a few steps away from the doors when my gaze snagged on an unexpected figure just outside the doors. Was that... *Summer*?

I hadn't been planning on going all the way out of the building without the guys, but the sight of my best friend had me pushing past the doors onto the campus sidewalk.

It was her. "Summer?" I said in disbelief as she turned toward me. Her lips were pursed, and her eyes seemed somehow sad. And then Mom and Holand moved into view behind her.

What the hell was going on? My gaze jerked from them back to Summer. "What are you doing here?"

I started to take a step back toward the doors, but Summer caught my wrist. "We need to talk, Madds. I told you this was getting out of hand. I came all the way out here for a reason."

I shook my head. "You shouldn't have. You know I can't—"

I was so distracted by the figures in front of me that I didn't notice the form approaching from behind until arms slammed around my waist and chest.

Someone heaved me up, and another man bent to snatch my ankles. A hand clapped over my mouth before I could let out more than a squeak of protest.

Without a second's hesitation, my captors hauled me to a van parked next to the curb and carried me straight through the open back doors.

CHAPTER
TWENTY-ONE

Dexter

"Let's get moving," Logan barked, as quietly as a person could bark in consideration of the space we were in. I'd already grabbed my book bag from where it'd been sitting near my feet while I dug through articles on the computer. Slinging the strap over my shoulder, I hurried after him and Slade, just a step behind them.

"What's happening?" I asked. "Is Madelyn okay?" He hadn't filled us in on any of the details yet, just announced that something was going down and we needed to get home.

Logan nodded curtly. "She went ahead to the front doors. We'll catch up with her there. Something bad's going down with Beckett, and I guess he's not sure if it'll affect us too. She also figured out something about the case—but we can get into that after we're home and—"

Both he and Slade stopped in their tracks so abruptly that I stepped on the heel of Slade's shoe. I pushed myself backward with a hurried apology and glanced past them to see four police officers in full uniform marching through the library toward us. A librarian was scurrying along beside them.

I only had a second to wonder what the cops might be here about when the librarian caught sight of us and pointed a finger directly at us.

Logan cursed under his breath and spun around, Slade following suit. As one being, we dashed in the opposite direction even as one of the cops let out a shout. "You three—stay where you are!"

"Fucking Doom's Seed must have sicced them on us," Logan groused, veering around a row of bookcases to hide us briefly from view. "Who knows what trumped up charges his people invented to pin us with."

Slade let out a rough chuckle. "That prick is really getting on my nerves."

My heart sank. It could be even worse than they were implying. We'd done a hell of a lot of illegal things in the past few years, not least of which was *murder*. It'd be a little hard to prove that the few deaths on our hands had been in self-defense now.

How much did our enemies know about our past crimes? Was this just a distraction, or had they found a potential way to destroy us without having to do any of the dirty work themselves?

We all knew that if we let ourselves be caught, it might be game over. Prison time, or at the very least trapped in a holding cell for who knew how long. We couldn't let that happen, not when the same psychos who'd arranged this were gunning for Madelyn.

Oh, hell, where was Madelyn? Had the assholes sent someone else after her?

There wasn't time to check. The thump of running footsteps carried from behind us. All we could think about was avoiding capture if we wanted to be around to protect Madelyn after this.

We hustled around the end of the aisle, and I spotted an exit sign farther down the wall up ahead, its glow dimmed.

"There!" I said, pointing, and pushed myself faster. My pulse was thudding so hard I could practically feel it in my feet as they pounded against the carpeted floor.

The sign was over a secluded stairwell with a plaque that said MAINTENANCE ONLY. We ignored that and pushed past the door. As it banged shut in our wake, we rushed down the stairs we found on the other side.

"Any idea where we're going, Dex?" Slade asked in a tone that wasn't demanding, only curious.

"Away from the cops. That seemed like the right direction."

Logan let out a huff of agreement. "We can figure out the rest later."

The stairwell ended at a basement level with another door. We shoved that open and came out into a dreary gray hallway that looked like it stretched forever into the distance.

"Let's get more of a head start on them," Logan said, propelling himself forward. "They'll probably figure out which way we headed before too long."

A sickly smell of industrial cleaner hung in the air, and pipes groaned somewhere in the distance. The florescent lights overhead flickered. Slade glanced up at them and grimaced. "Feels like a scene out of a horror movie."

"There have to be other exits," I said. "We just have to find one and get out."

Several other halls branched off from the one we were in. Logan took the first left and then a right at the next branch. The walls and floors looked identical with every turn. Through a couple of doors that stood ajar, I spotted dusty plastic storage bins and cardboard boxes.

"Seems like everything the university doesn't have a use for anymore is stashed down here," Logan said.

It definitely didn't look as if anyone had come by in quite a while, though the smell suggested that the janitorial staff had supplies down here too. The halls themselves appeared clean enough though eerie in atmosphere.

The sameness of the halls made it hard to keep track of our turns. I kept my ears pricked, but I couldn't make out any sounds of pursuit behind us. That didn't mean the cops weren't on their way, though.

"What do you think happened to Madelyn?" I asked.

Logan checked his phone and growled. "No signal down here, so no way to ask her—or let her know what happened to *us*. I hope we can get out of this fucking maze soon so we can find out. *She* hasn't been involved in anything major. The cops can't have anything real on her."

She had been with us at the warehouse where we'd ended up killing the two thugs in self-defense, though. And she'd come with us into more than one building where I'd picked the lock so we could enter. He couldn't know for sure they didn't have evidence of that.

A sense of gloom descended over me, making my stomach clench. The seemingly endless halls only added to my growing uneasiness. What if there *wasn't* another exit after all?

Another doubt crept up so insistently that I couldn't help saying it out loud. "Maybe we shouldn't have run. If they catch us now, we'll end up in even more trouble than if we'd talked to them and tried to address whatever they were concerned about. We had no idea what they actually wanted to talk to us about."

Logan shook his head. "No way. Everyone knows you don't talk to cops unless you have to. Especially when they look like they're ready to break out the handcuffs already. They'll grab at any reason to pin something on you so they can call the case closed."

"And we have no idea what they have on us—or think they have," Slade put in. "Given what this Doom's

Seed psycho has pulled off already, I wouldn't put much of anything past him." He paused. "Of course, we're screwed no matter what if we can't find another way out of here without getting caught."

What would happen if we ended up confronting the cops down here? Did Logan have that gun he'd gotten from the chop shop on him? Would we end up in some kind of shoot-out—become cop-killers on top of everything else?

I could feel my thoughts spiraling into a panic, but I couldn't seem to rein them in. A shiver ran down my back as visions of sprawled, bloody bodies flashed through my mind. Like that first one—that night at the abandoned strip mall when I'd—

"Hey." Slade came around in front of me where I couldn't avoid looking at him, his voice softening. "I was just kidding around. I know we'll figure this out. And even if the situation gets worse, we're in this together, right?"

My breath hitched. I couldn't stop myself from saying, "We're only in this because of me."

Logan knit his brow. "What are you talking about, Dex? You didn't have any idea those cops were coming after us, did you?"

"No. But—but everything leading up to that. All the things they could arrest us for. All the things we did…" I pressed the heel of my hand to my forehead, but the pressure barely took the edge off the emotions whirling through me.

If this was a puzzle, then I knew exactly which piece

made the key part of the picture. And I'd put it there. Two and a half years ago, that guy had lunged at us out of nowhere with a switchblade and stabbed Slade in the shoulder, and I'd sliced into him so automatically with the first rush of protective adrenaline. In just a couple of seconds, it'd been like he wasn't even human anymore, just a collection of fleshy parts that my mind narrowed down to its most vulnerable points.

What kind of person was I if I could reduce any human being to an object to be broken and destroyed?

"I'm pretty sure we were all there for all the things we did," Slade said, but a thread of worry wove through his joking tone.

I folded my arms over my chest. "It was me. The first time we went from guys just unraveling mysteries and tripping up the criminals to actually *murdering* someone. Maybe I didn't need to kill him. I put all that blood on our hands, and then nothing was too much. We just kept heading farther down that path."

Logan sucked in a breath. "Dex, man, you can't blame yourself for that. You were fucking amazing that night. If you hadn't jumped in there so fast, that asshole might have murdered *Slade*. We've all had to make the same call."

"But I started it. I set it all in motion."

"Dex," Slade said firmly. I could feel him peering into my eyes even though I couldn't handle the direct eye contact right now, my gaze fixed on his shirt collar. "It was going to happen sometime. Logan and I know that, one hundred percent. We were getting into more dangerous stuff already, more aggressive crimes, more hardened criminals… If it hadn't been then, it would have happened a little later anyway. I swear to God, it's not on you."

I'd never heard Slade Galvezo sound that serious. My eyes twitched upward to briefly meet his. He looked serious too, serious and solemn and like he'd have killed for *me* right now if he needed to, no questions asked.

"Have you really been thinking that way all this time?" Logan asked. "Like it's your fault that we've gotten so far off the straight and narrow?"

"Of course," I mumbled. It'd seemed obvious.

A ragged laugh spilled out of him. "I've always thought it was *my* fault. Pushing us to go farther and take on more intense problems. Digging into the stuff with Maddie's dad."

My gaze slid to him, my forehead furrowing. "Of course it isn't your fault."

Slade gave me a brief, light clap on the shoulder, careful not to let it linger. "And that's exactly what we're telling you, dude. It sounds just as ridiculous to us as Logan blaming himself." He raised an eyebrow at Logan. "For the record, I do also think your theory is ridiculous."

Logan gave him a baleful look. "Thanks so much for weighing in."

Their easy banter brought me back to earth. I inhaled slowly, and my nerves seemed to settle.

Could they be right? It wasn't really my fault but

just a natural consequence of the general path we'd all agreed to go down?

I'd never seen it that way before, but maybe I hadn't let myself. I couldn't deny that it made a certain amount of sense, especially the way the other guys talked about it.

A soft glow washed through my chest, soothing parts of my spirit that I hadn't known were so bruised. It was okay. I'd protected my friend, saved his life. We were where we'd already been heading.

Trying out those thoughts, they felt okay. Maybe even right.

I glanced around the hallways again. We *had* been in much direr situations than this before, and I'd helped us get out of plenty of them. If I got my head on straight, I could handle this too. The path we took now was what really mattered.

Logan had called the halls a maze. A maze was a kind of puzzle. I should be the perfect person to crack its visual code.

"Let's keep going," I said. "I haven't been paying enough attention. I need to take a closer look at everything down here."

My friends started walking without question, trusting my process. That was the trust I'd earned from them over the past several years. We walked straight for a few minutes, then took another turn with me in the lead, then another.

My attention narrowed down to the small labels I hadn't given much thought to at first. They were meaningless at first glance, combinations of letters and numbers like L4 and P2, but every corner was marked with them.

And the pipes we'd heard humming… I cocked my head, absorbing the sound, and moved toward it. After another couple of turns, we came to a section of hall where a few thick pipes stretched along one side of the ceiling.

Studying them, a mental map of the university campus unfolded in my mind. I pointed to the pipes. "I think those lead to the library bathrooms. All the L labels are that way, and they must stand for Library. Which means that must be the western end of the building." I swiveled on my heel and motioned in the other direction. "So, this is east. And P must stand for something else. The PhysEd facilities are just east of the library, aren't they?"

Slade let out an awed whistle. "I have no sense of direction, but if you say it is, I believe it."

"The basements for some of the campus buildings are connected," I said with growing excitement. "Which means they must all have access points. Let's get back to the nearest P hall and see where we can go from there."

A bang of a door somewhere in the distance had us striding forward faster, trying to keep our footsteps as quiet as possible. We hurried down the first hall with a P label, and I scanned all the side halls we passed. Where had I noticed stairwells in the PhysEd building? To the left of the main entrance, and near the back, which relative to the library, would be right around…

I turned at another hall and spotted a door at the end of it.

Slade let out a near-silent whoop of approval and saluted me. "That's our Dex. Couldn't make it through any of this shit without you."

We hustled down the hall and were relieved to find the door opened no problem. It was a matter of seconds before we were stepping out in the humid air of a first-floor hall near the swimming pool. Logan smiled, now knowing exactly where we were—and how to get out of here—just as I did.

"We've got to get off campus," he said, and pulled out his phone. His smile fell away. "No texts from Maddie. If she's okay, she'd be wondering where we are."

He tapped in a quick message as we hurried to the front doors. I listened for the ping of a text in reply, but nothing came. My stomach knotted all over again.

We eased out of the PhysEd building and peeked around the corner toward the front of the library. A few students were walking in and out, but none of them were Madelyn. I couldn't make out her blond hair beyond the windows in the doors. And a police car was parked a few spaces down. We couldn't go back into the library without being seen.

Logan sucked a breath through his teeth with a hiss. He looked at his phone again, but the screen had remained blank.

We'd gotten to relative safety—but what the hell did we do now?

CHAPTER
TWENTY-TWO

Madelyn

I landed on my ass inside the back of the van with an audible *oof*. The doors banged shut, and I whirled around to find myself staring at my mom, Summer, and…

"Lee?" I snapped in disbelief, my gaze jerking from one of the guys who'd grabbed me to the other. "Eric?"

As Holland climbed into the front of the van and started the engine, the two guys made nearly identical sheepish expressions. I hadn't seen my cousins—sons of Mom's older brother—since Christmas, which was pretty much the only time I ever saw them since they'd gotten old enough to move out on their own several years ago.

"What the hell is going on here?" I demanded, my gaze veering from them to Mom.

"I'm so sorry, sweetie," Mom said in a cajoling voice, her eyes clouded with concern. "I didn't know what else to do. We've gotten so worried about you, and you wouldn't talk to me or Summer. Having a full intervention was a last resort."

Oh my God. I glared at Eric, the slightly older of the two guys. "And you thought dragging me off the street into the back of a van was a good idea?"

He held up his hands in surrender. "Aunt Lindsay gave a convincing story. We were just doing what she asked."

A growl escaped me. I looked to Summer next. "I can't believe you went along with this. I *told* you I could handle everything."

Before she could answer, my phone pinged with an incoming text. I reached to answer it, but Summer plucked it right out of my hand and shoved it into her back pocket.

"No way," she said. "You shouldn't be talking to anyone but us right now. Especially not Logan."

"What are you talking about? Logan hasn't done anything wrong."

Her lips pursed. "I know what you've said, Maddie, but it's also been obvious that something big is going on, something that's freaked you out, and he's mixed up in it somehow. It seems like he's gotten inside your head and dragged you into something dangerous. Just come clean about what's going on, and we'll figure out how to help you."

The van shifted with a turn, and I had to brace my hand against the wall to stop myself from sliding on the carpeted floor. My stomach was tying itself into knots.

Had the text been from the Vigil guys, wondering why I'd disappeared? Or from Beckett with another update about the escalation in his conflict with Doom's Seed? I had no idea what might be happening to any of the guys I cared about right now, and they'd start panicking if they couldn't get a hold of me.

I needed to get out of this situation.

"There's nothing to come clean about," I said in as firm a voice as I could muster. "Nothing's going on. I have class in half an hour—you're going to force me to mess up my education now? Why don't we stop this and I'll meet you for a regular dinner or something tonight?"

I'd thought that leaning on the education thing was the right call since Mom knew what my dream career meant to me, but her expression didn't budge. "We're doing this now. The sooner you start opening up, the sooner we can resolve this."

"Who knows if you'd even show up for dinner or anything else if we let you go," Summer muttered.

The words stung even though they were completely true. I'd tossed out that offering only to escape the intervention—I doubted I'd be any more ready to spill my guts tonight than I was at the moment. I gritted my teeth.

"You know, kidnapping is illegal," I told them. "You could get arrested for this."

Summer gave me her best "bitch please" look, which I guessed was fair since I was totally bluffing. I wouldn't have called the cops on her or Mom and Holland—Lee and Eric, I didn't have as many qualms about—and even if I would have, I didn't have anything to call them *with*. I was stuck.

"It doesn't matter how bad it is," she said. "You've got to fess up. That's the only way this is ending."

"This is ridiculous," I told her, and then my mouth stayed clamped shut.

The van jolted over a pothole, turned, and rumbled to a stop. Mom nodded to my cousins, who stood up. I pushed to my feet too and peered through the windows on the back doors.

We were parked outside the room at the end of a motel, a tarnished brass number 9 mounted on the yellow door.

I wrinkled my nose. "You're kidding me."

"We can do this in there or stay in the van," Mom said firmly.

I weighed my options and decided I'd rather take my chances in the motel room. There might be an emergency exit of some sort. I'd at least have more room to maneuver. Here in the back of the van, I was completely trapped.

"Fine."

My cousins marched me into the motel room with the others following behind. When Holand had closed the door and turned the deadbolt, Lee and Eric positioned themselves in front of it like bouncers. I glowered at them again and dropped onto the edge of the bed.

The comforter was a mottled grey, the carpet patchy navy. A faint smell of mildew hung in the air. Delightful. The yellow door was the only cheerful thing in this place.

"I still don't know what you want me to say," I insisted. "There's nothing to confess. I've been busy with school and extracurricular stuff, and I didn't want to stress you out by complaining. And I just haven't had much time to talk in general."

Summer snorted. "I've known you since elementary school, Madds. I can tell when you're lying. But I think this is the first time you've ever lied this blatantly to my face. You've been dodging the truth for weeks now."

Holand stepped up beside her, his expression so solemn that guilt started gnawing at my gut. "Maddie, you know your mother and I have always tried to give you and Logan plenty of freedom to live your lives. But if something's gone wrong for one or both of you—and it definitely seems like it has—we need to know. You're still our children."

I swallowed thickly. "What exactly do *you* think Logan's done?"

His mouth pulled with a grimace. "I don't know. I don't want to believe anything negative about him, but he's been so withdrawn for years now… It's hard not to wonder what secrets he might have been keeping."

"He has a right to secrets, doesn't he? We both do. We're grown-ups now; we don't need to share every detail of our lives with you."

Holand winced. "Of course you don't. But if Logan's gotten into some kind of trouble and mixed you up in it too, I want to know—so I can help both of you. That's all I want to do: help, however you need it."

Mom nodded emphatically and reached for my hand, wincing when I scooted away from her. "Refusing to talk to us only makes me more sure that whatever you've gotten into, it's very serious. Please, Maddie. Don't keep shutting us out like this."

My stomach clenched even tighter. They didn't understand. They didn't realize that there was *nothing* they could do to help. Having them separate from this mess and safer because of their distance helped me more than anything they could have offered if they'd known the truth.

But then, that *was* exactly the way Logan had thought about me—his reason for keeping me in the dark for so long. He hadn't believed I'd be able to help all that much, but I had. We'd gotten so much closer to unraveling the mystery because of what I knew.

In some ways, that was different. I'd known Dad so well, and I'd been with him when he'd died. No one else in the motel room with me could have had any idea about what he'd gotten mixed up in before his death except for Mom, and I already knew how far our enemies would go to hurt her.

Next time it might be fatal, the text I'd gotten after her accident had said.

But how could I get out of this intervention without dragging them all into the line of fire? The motel room had given me a little breathing room, but I was still just as stuck as I'd been in the van.

"You know how stubborn I can be, Maddie," Summer said, folding her arms over her chest. "You're not winning this—other than I think talking to us will be better for you in the long run anyway. I don't care how crazy things are; I just want to know what's happened to my best friend."

The guilt I'd felt earlier expanded through my chest. It was with Summer where I'd screwed up the most. Mom would have accepted me being a little distant, because I hadn't talked to her *that* much to begin with, and Holand had put up with Logan's anti-social behavior for years. But I'd almost completely frozen out the friend who'd always been there for me. No matter what excuses I gave, that'd been unfair.

And it'd come back to bite me in the ass. If I'd opened up to her, she wouldn't have gotten so worried she'd compared stories with my mom. No intervention, no sitting here in this dank motel room wondering what fresh hell might be descending on my boyfriends. Maybe she'd have understood without pushing herself into harm's way on my behalf. She'd at least have realized why I couldn't simply walk away.

"I really think this was taking the situation to a huge extreme," I had to say. "Going this far... How am

I supposed to trust you if you'd grab me and haul me off like this?"

A liquid shimmer entered Mom's eyes. "You need to trust that we're only doing this because of how much we care about you, Madelyn. Because it matters this much to us to make sure that you're okay—or that you'll be okay, at least."

I did know that. But I also knew that telling her and Holand about Dad's murder wouldn't just paint targets on their backs—it could destroy our chances of getting real answers too. They'd insist on going straight to the police with what we already knew, the police would interfere with the investigation the Vigil guys and Beckett were already immersed with, who knew what would happen to Beckett's family if the spotlight was turned on them…

No. Too much was at stake.

But I could take a different gamble. It might be the only chance I had. And I owed it to her.

I glanced at Summer and then at my mom. "Can I just chat with Summer for a little while? It's a lot of pressure, having you all hanging over me. It might be easier to hash things out one on one."

Mom hesitated, but hope had lit in her eyes. "I think that might be a good first step."

She looked at Holand, who nodded slowly. "We could go and pick up some lunch for everyone while you two talk," he suggested.

Mom wagged a finger at me. "But you're staying in this room until we're all clear on what you've been hiding from us." She beckoned to my cousins. "You two can wait outside the door. Make sure Madelyn doesn't try to leave."

Lee and Eric dipped their heads obediently. Eric shot me an apologetic grimace before they all headed out.

Summer flopped onto the bed a couple of feet from me and grimaced as she examined the comforter. "I'm not sure it's really safe to be making surface contact with anything in this place. Ugh." Her attention homed in on me. "So are you actually going to talk, or was that just an attempt at tricking your way out of this?"

My throat tightened. "I'm sorry, Summer. I really am. I know I've said that before, but I meant it all those times too."

She raised her chin. "Sorry doesn't matter much if you're just going to pull the same bullshit as before."

"No. I'm going to talk to you properly now. I probably should have before." I rubbed my forehead. "I'm still worried that you'll get dragged into the danger too, but... but I guess that's your choice to make, like it was for me. I'm just asking that you listen the whole way through before you make any decisions. I still feel like I need to keep Mom and Holand out of this."

Summer's expression was skeptical, but she motioned for me to go on. "I'm listening."

God, how did I even start? I groped for the right words. "You know my car got stolen a couple of months ago, and that's how I ended up talking to Logan again."

She snapped her fingers. "I *knew* he was involved in this."

I gave her a pointed look, and she closed her mouth with a zipping gesture.

"Yeah," I said, "but I doubt it's in any way you could have guessed. It turned out my car getting stolen wasn't random. It also turns out... you know how Logan and his friends have been investigating all those petty crimes on campus? They've gotten into more serious situations too. And a few years ago, they started finding evidence that my dad didn't really get sick—he was murdered. Poisoned somehow."

Summer's jaw dropped. "You're serious?"

I exhaled in a rush. "Yeah. It took me ages to be sure of it myself, but I've seen enough now that I know it's true. But the evidence we've turned up, it's not solid enough that we could take it to the police and expect them to investigate a crime that's not even recorded as a crime and that happened over a decade ago. We've been trying to find enough proof to get to that point, and... the people responsible have realized we've been investigating. They caused my mom's accident, among other things."

"Holy shit." Summer's eyes looked ready to pop out of her head.

"So that's why I've been so hesitant to tell any of you about it," I went on in a rush. "I didn't want them to target anyone else I care about. We've been laying as low as we can in the hopes that they'll think *we* aren't even investigating any more… It's gotten pretty complicated."

"This—this is huge." Summer shook her head. "You should have told me, Maddie. You know I'd want to have your back no matter what."

I hung my head. "Like I said, I'm sorry. You have no idea how much I mean that. Logan made the same mistake with me, you know. He ghosted me because he was afraid if we got closer, I'd find out about the investigation, and he was trying to keep *me* safe."

Summer sputtered a laugh. "That makes a very weird kind of sense." She pinched the bridge of her nose. "Don't you think your mom should know too, at least? He was her husband."

"They've already left her injured, maybe even permanently. And you know she'd say we have to let the police handle it. I might end up on total lockdown if she knew I want to keep digging myself. But I can't let this go, Summer. I need to get justice for my dad. His murderers have been walking free for years… He didn't deserve what they did to him. And the guys and I might be the only people who can fix it, as much as it can be fixed."

"Okay. I get that. I still wish you'd told me sooner, but I guess this is better than you being hooked on meth or something." She sighed. "So, now what?"

I gave her a beseeching look. "So, now's your chance to really help me. We were *so* close to putting the pieces together. We'd just figured out one major clue when you guys grabbed me. But I can't see it through while I'm stuck here in this 'intervention.' I need to get out of here. This is going to be my best chance to prove Dad was murdered—maybe my last chance."

Her jaw tightened, and I thought she was going to argue more. But instead she pushed closer on the bed and wrapped her arms around me in a hug.

"You're always taking so much on your shoulders, Madds. You need to let other people carry some of the burden."

"I'm trying to do that now," I said quietly.

She groaned and gave me another squeeze before letting me go. "All right. I'll help you take off. I don't think you should be putting yourself in all that danger… but I get why you feel you need to, and if I'm going to ask you to trust me, then I've got to trust you to make your own decisions too."

Relief flooded me. I grinned at her, momentarily lost for words. "Thank you," I managed finally.

She pointed a finger at me. "I do have a condition. No more keeping me in the dark. If it seems like you're in danger and hiding things from me again, I'm going to tell your mom everything. No second chances."

I couldn't even say that was unfair. "Absolutely. It'll be my fault if you feel you have to go that far. But hopefully this will all be resolved in a few days, and then I can tell Mom everything anyway."

"I'll keep my fingers crossed." She studied me for a moment. "Are you sure there isn't anything else I can do right now?"

"I swear I'd tell you if there was," I said. "And if

something comes up that I know you could pitch in on, I'll tell you. Either way, I'll be keeping you in the loop."

"Okay. Let's do this, then." She dug into her pockets and handed me my phone and a car key. "That's for my Mazda—it's parked opposite the van. Please be careful with her. I want to hear from you within a few hours so I know where to pick her up. Now, to deal with your cousins…"

She rubbed her hands together, and a familiar gleam came into her eyes. I couldn't help smiling. This was the Summer I loved.

"Got it," she announced, and motioned to the door. "Stand back there. I'll get them to rush in, and you duck out while I'm distracting them."

I got into position behind where the door would open. Summer walked over to close the bathroom and then marched past me to yank the front door open.

"Oh my God!" she babbled. "You guys have got to help me! Maddie went and locked herself in the bathroom, and the sounds coming from in there—I don't know what she's doing, but it can't be good."

The panic in her voice must have convinced my cousins. They came barreling into the room after her, rushing to the bathroom.

I whipped past the door and sprinted across the parking lot. The gold Mazda unlocked with a beep. Diving into the driver's seat, I started the engine. Then, with a silent thank you to my bestie and any other powers that might be, I turned the car back toward the center of the city and hit the gas.

CHAPTER
TWENTY-THREE

Madelyn

The hole-in-the-wall cafe on the other side of town smelled of strong coffee beans with an undertone of stale sweat. I stared down at the coffee I'd received from the overly perky teen at the counter and debated whether or not I should actually drink it.

Slade chugged his without any apparent concern about the cleanliness or burning his tongue, and followed it with one of his cinnamon candies. Dexter was eying his mug with a trepidation that looked similar to what I felt.

Logan hadn't even bothered to order. He sat down at the rickety table near the front window, got up again, paced a couple of steps, and then forced himself back into his chair, looking like he wanted to march out there and drag Beckett to the meeting we'd managed to arrange after I'd called the guys.

After I'd gotten away from my mom and best friend's intervention. Which Slade wasn't finished heckling me about yet.

He shook his head at me with a teasing tsk of his tongue. "Look at you. Such an addict. Keeping such bad company that your parents had to do an intervention from your own stepbrother, and you came running right back to us the first second you could."

I rolled my eyes at him. "They probably thought I was on drugs or something."

"Or that Logan was pimping you out." Slade cocked his head as if considering that possibility.

"Shut up," Logan grumbled. "It's ridiculous."

"It's hilarious."

Dexter made a face. "It does make sense that they'd have been suspicious. Madelyn's change in behavior must have seemed pretty extreme."

I sighed. "Well, now we'll just have to hope that Summer can hold them at bay long enough for us to get what we need." I'd texted her when I'd left her car to join the guys in an Uber, but I hadn't had anything else to report to her yet, and she hadn't replied.

Logan looked as if he might have groused more, but right then the door to the café chimed. Beckett walked in with a glance around the place, wearing his more incognito clothing of jeans and a hoodie. His hair looked unusually rumpled beneath the raised hood.

He was the one who'd suggested this place for the meetup, confident that no cops were likely to cruise by on their regular patrols. I wasn't sure I wanted to find out how he knew that information so well, but it'd worked out. I still couldn't believe that the Vigil guys had needed to go on the run from the police in the short time I'd been gone.

He walked over to us as steady as always, but I could see the tension in every movement. I couldn't help checking him over for injuries as well as I could, but there were no signs of blood on his clothes or pain in his expression.

"What happened?" I said in a hushed voice as soon as he reached our table. "Did you get Doom's Seed's people to back off?"

He shook his head with a frown. "The attack's still on-going. I can't stay for long. But I wasn't accomplishing much at the moment anyway, so at least I can make sure the four of you are safe."

"What do you mean, under attack?" Dexter asked before Beckett could go on, leaning forward.

Beckett exhaled sharply. "Armed men stormed several of the Storm-owned businesses in the city— including the dance club, the trucking company, and my new office complex. It's obvious that they were looking to get in quietly and simply slaughter everyone working for me, but thankfully my people are alert and noticed some odd behavior. They were able to get out a warning to the others just in time to be on the defense."

My stomach had sunk. "What's happening now?"

"Everyone barricaded themselves in the buildings. But it's hard on the ground levels that have storefronts with big windows. They've ended up holed up in back rooms or basements where they can't maneuver easily. I've been talking to people at each location, and it sounds like most of them have survived so far, but they're under siege. They can't leave without getting shot, and they can't get good shots in at the people who've invaded."

Logan's brow furrowed. "And you don't have enough people who aren't trapped to fight back from the outside?"

Beckett grimaced. "My family has a lot of resources and people, but they're spread out. This has severely limited who I can call on in the area. I'm rallying everyone I can who isn't stuck, but I'm not sure if there's much we can do other than wait it out. If we get into a full shoot-out at all of my businesses, it's going to draw so much unwanted police attention... That could destroy our holdings in the city in itself. It'd be a total bloodbath."

My eyebrows shot up, the guys' account of their escape from the police racing through my mind. "Couldn't you use the police to scare off Doom's Seed's people? If they're actively firing illegal weapons and making a commotion..."

"They *haven't* been able to do all that much shooting so far, not so much that the police have been called in. These aren't residential neighborhoods. Unless they see something they can't ignore, people in the city tend to stay out of any kind of conflict."

"*You* could call the cops in," Slade pointed out with a click of his candy against his teeth.

Beckett aimed a baleful look at him. "And that really wouldn't help my concerns about police interference with my businesses, would it? They could just as easily end up shooting *my* people as the assholes attacking us."

My mind worked through the problem. Doom's Seed wouldn't want his people detained and questioned any more than Beckett did. And the cops didn't have to go right at them for the criminals to get worried. From what they'd said, the Vigil guys had gone on the alert as soon as they'd spotted the cops in the library.

"What if… what if you didn't point them at your businesses at all," I said slowly. "As long as the attackers *think* the police are going to show up and arrest them, they won't stick around, right?"

Beckett raised his eyebrows. "How would we make them think that if it's not true?"

"Give them something else to investigate. Like… 'symptoms' of a problem nearby that'll draw a whole lot of police attention, close enough that it'll spook Doom's Seed's men but not focused on any property you own."

Slade tapped his hand on the table. "I like that. Maddie bringing her doctor training to the task in creative ways."

Beckett's eyes glazed for a few seconds as he

contemplated my suggestion. He was just opening his mouth when his phone rang.

He jerked it to his ear. "Yes?" Then his expression lightened. He stood a little straighter, nodding. "Excellent. You have an address? Send me all the information."

My heart leapt. But as Beckett hung up, his expression got more serious again.

He looked around at us. "That was one of my tech guys. He's identified a location on the outskirts of the city where some of the 'toxic' fish were shipped regularly but that doesn't appear to be a restaurant or any other business you'd expect to be ordering raw fish. He isn't sure *what* it is."

Logan's eyes widened. "That's the lead we need. But —you need to deal with this gang war you've got on your hands first."

Beckett swiped his hand over his mouth. "I do. But you know what—I think Maddie's plan just might work if I put the right spin on it. It reminds me of some strategies that got us pretty far back in Paradise Bend."

I smiled. "Then let's do it."

"*I* am going to do most of it," Beckett said firmly, and paused. "But you four had better come with me. If the police are going to be racing around the city, I want to be sure you're out of their way. And as soon as this is dealt with, we'll investigate this place and its toxic fish."

As I pressed the dial button, my gaze stayed trained on the street beyond the van's tinted back window. Beckett had gone off in that direction after we'd parked not far from his office complex. He'd texted me seconds ago telling me to go ahead with my part in the plan. I just hoped this worked, since it'd technically been my idea.

The line on the other end rang, and then a crisp professional voice answered, telling me I'd reached the police department.

"I have a crime to report," I said quickly. "I was at the Lotus Blossom Spa a couple of days ago, and I saw them selling baggies of drugs out of a back room."

"Hold on a second." There was a rustling sound on the other end. "What exactly did you see?"

I improvised on the spot, wanting to make sure they took the accusation seriously. "A couple of people gave the staff money and were handed baggies of this white powder. I saw one of them snort some of it. It was obviously making them high."

"And this is the Lotus Blossom Spa at Trinity and Highland?"

"Yes."

"All right. Can I get your name for—"

I hung up, leaving the tip anonymous. A sweat had broken out over my back, but Slade patted my shoulder reassuringly. "Nice work."

We'd decided that sending the police to some of the businesses in Doom's Seed's empire would add to the chaos and make him more likely to pull all his men out of their siege. But that was only one small part of the plan.

As for the other part…

Beckett hurried back to the van just as I was pushing my phone into my pocket. He hopped inside, slightly windblown, yanked the door shut, and pushed a button on the small rectangular device he was holding.

I knew what was coming, but that didn't stop me from flinching at the boom that reverberated through the air. A surge of fire exploded through a car parked across the street from the office complex. The roof burst open; the windows shattered. My ears rang with the noise.

"Too bad for the owner of that car," I had to say.

Beckett glanced at me with a mild expression. "His insurance will cover it. And anyway, I've met the guy who owns it, and he's an asshole."

Logan barked a laugh. "All's well that ends well, huh?"

"It's not over yet."

We sat, tensed, as the fire roared inside the car. All across the city, Beckett's people had staged similar explosions near the businesses under siege. They were being timed so that the cops weren't stretched too thin, but close together enough to make it clear there was an urgent problem.

Within minutes, incoming sirens wailed. Three police cars sped onto the scene. They parked around the burning car and leapt out.

As they stalked around the car and then started

checking the nearby stores for signs of the perpetrator, a couple of figures emerged from the side door of the office complex. We'd specifically parked where we could keep watch, because Beckett had said that was where the attackers had broken into the building.

The two men eyed the cops and jerked back when one of the officers started striding in the direction of the office complex. They ducked back inside. My pulse stuttered with the fear that they'd hide out inside and go unnoticed. But seconds later, about a dozen figures hustled out and rushed down the alley to make their getaway.

Beckett sucked in a breath. "Lindell's with them. I'm not letting him get away with this."

He sprang past us into the driver's seat and started the engine. The van roared around and swerved down a side street. Logan gripped my arm to help hold me in place in the back.

I had no idea where Beckett thought he was going until he roared around another bend—and slammed on the brakes just shy of hitting a car that'd been about to pull away from the curb.

A tall man with bushy eyebrows and a heavy layer of graying stubble stared out the driver's side window at him. I guessed that was Lindell. He reached for his door, but it banged into the van's front bumper, too close for him to squeeze out.

By then, Beckett had already pushed out of the van, a pistol in his hand. Logan lunged out after him, yanking out his own gun. My stomach twisted, but we all followed.

The stubbled man froze as Beckett and Logan circled the car. Beckett waved the gun at him. "Get the fuck out, Lindell. I've got a lot of questions I need to ask you."

Lindell looked like he was attempting a smirk, but his expression was so tense it came out sour. "Nice to see you again, Storm's heir."

"What are we doing?" I hissed as Lindell eased out of the vehicle through the passenger side.

"He knows *all* about his boss's business," Beckett said, checking the man over for weapons. He pulled a gun out of a hidden holster and tossed it into the back of the car. "He might be able to give us some answers about where we're going next."

He tipped his head toward the other guys by the van without taking his eyes off his enemy. "There's rope in my glove compartment. Get it. We don't want to leave this prick mobile for our little trip."

CHAPTER
TWENTY-FOUR

Madelyn

The address Beckett had gotten turned out to be an ordinary-looking storefront with plain beige walls, a shade drawn over the dingy front window, and a logo-less sign that simply proclaimed the place to be "Teresa's."

"Teresa's what?" Slade muttered, peering at it. "Convenience store? Shoe shop? Hat boutique?"

"No way of finding out without going in. All I know for sure is they don't receive any other food or animal related deliveries." Beckett got out of the driver's seat and walked around to the back doors. He untied Lindell from the bar he'd secured him to and removed the ropes around his ankles as well, leaving his hands tied behind his back.

"Come on," he said. "You can give us the tour and tell us all about what goes on in this place. And if there's anyone inside, you'll make a handy shield."

Lindell grimaced around the strip of fabric that gagged him, but he went with Beckett without any further struggle. He didn't appear to be too concerned about ending up in the middle of a gun fight here, but I followed cautiously.

Logan pushed ahead of me, taking out his gun again. The sight of it made my stomach turn, but I couldn't deny that it'd been useful. I wasn't going to tell him to put it away until we'd seen what was waiting for us in this place.

The guys had fallen into a more cohesive comradery over the past several days. Beckett kept one hand on Lindell's arm and tipped his head to Logan, who rapped on the door. When no one answered, he tried the doorknob. It didn't budge.

Dexter was already there with his lock picks. "I can handle that."

His deft fingers and the tools made quick work of the lock. He pushed the door open and poked his head inside. "No alarm system."

Slade smiled thinly. "Because whatever they're doing in here, they don't want any outside security company finding out about it, I bet."

Beckett and Logan entered first, nudging Doom's Seed's lieutenant in front of them. The room we walked into held nothing but a small metal desk at one end and a single chair at the other. The linoleum floor was covered with scuff marks, and a sour chemical smell laced the air that reminded me of the hospital.

Beckett hummed to himself. "My guy said they only get deliveries from the market once or twice a month. Maybe they don't bother to have anyone manning the place in between whatever it is they do with those."

He pushed Lindell onward through the doorway at the other end of the entry room. This space was larger, with a few padded chairs along one wall and an exam table set up at the far end next to a couple of counters and cabinets. It looks like a combined waiting room and medical exam room. It was as empty and silent as the front area, the sour smell thickening.

Dexter walked to another door off to the side and peeked in there. "More medical stuff," he reported. "No one there, no other entrances. The place is empty."

"Good," Beckett said. "Then we can talk."

He shoved Lindell down onto one of the chairs and bent to attach his bound wrists to the back of the chair. He fixed both ankles to the legs with plastic ties as well.

Watching him move so confidently and efficiently sent a chilly tingle down my back. He knew exactly what he was doing. How many people had he interrogated before?

How far would he take that interrogation if this guy didn't tell us what we needed to know?

But then, I'd already watched my other three guys beating up a security guard while they questioned him. Beckett would have to go pretty far to get more violent than that. The guy in front of us was involved in so many deaths and so much violence himself. I couldn't say I totally objected to him being on the receiving end if it helped us get justice for Dad.

When Lindell was securely bound to the chair, Beckett removed the gag. Lindell spat in his general direction and then glowered at him.

Beckett folded his arms over his chest. "You know we could do a lot worse to you than this. I caught you in the middle of an attack on one of my properties; you're lucky you're even still *alive*. The man you work for couldn't blame me for ending your sorry existence. But I'm giving you a chance to be useful instead."

"You'll forgive me if I don't thank you," Lindell rasped back.

Beckett continued as if he hadn't spoken. "Why did Doom's Seed attack the Storm's holdings in this city today?"

Lindell's lips curled with a sneer. "*He* didn't attack them. I did. Give credit where it's due."

So, he was going with the story that he was responsible for everything, that his boss hadn't even been aware and hadn't approved? I frowned, unconvinced.

From Beckett's tone, I suspected he wasn't either. "And why would *you* attack me?"

"To impress Doom's Seed," Lindell said without hesitation. "To show him how much I can do for him, how valuable I am. If I took the city all for us without him having to lift a finger, he could benefit without needing to take responsibility for it. That's the kind of loyalty he deserves."

Slade snorted. Logan was watching the conversation with narrowed eyes, his mouth pressed tight.

Beckett tapped his pistol against his thigh. "It wasn't just gaining territory you were interested in, though. You also went after four college students." He motioned to us. "You—or someone else under Doom's Seed—arranged for Lindsay Silver to have a car accident, and you burned down an office these three guys were using in the university law library. How about you tell me more about that?"

Lindell scoffed at him. "What's there to tell? They were poking around in the boss's business. It's *my* business to make sure he goes undisturbed. So I did what it took to shut them down."

His story felt way too pat for me. Too convenient that he bore responsibility for everything. Beckett had told me he didn't think Doom's Seed would allow any further attacks once Beckett had alerted him... unless he approved of them. He and this guy must have talked after Beckett had confronted Doom's Seed. It didn't add up.

But the gang war was lower on my list of concerns, especially seeing the medical equipment in the room. I took a step forward, and Beckett eased to the side, glancing at me. He gave me a slight nod as if to say I could take the floor.

A nervous shiver tickled through me. *I'd* never

interrogated anyone before. But I knew what I wanted to ask.

"You didn't shut us down," I said, glaring at Lindell. "And now we know so much more than we did before. What is your boss using this facility for? What was he having shipped here in the cold boxes from the seafood market? Viruses and bacteria? Experimental toxins?"

Lindell shook his head. His voice came out even harder than before. "I don't know anything about that. This isn't my part of the business."

Beckett made a skeptical noise. "You're his primary lieutenant in this metropolitan area, and you have no idea about major activities he was running here? Nice try. Why don't you take another stab at answering properly?"

"He keeps some things separate. It's his right to do that."

"And Evan Silver?" Dexter spoke up abruptly. "Why have you been so focused on covering up his death?"

"Who?" Lindell asked, blank-faced, but this time I was sure it was an act.

"You know who," I insisted. "The only thing we've been doing that could have pissed off your boss is trying to figure out why he was murdered. That's what you're covering up."

My show of temper only seemed to make the lieutenant more confident. He shrugged. "You broke into properties under his purview. You were hassling people under him. It doesn't matter to me why; it needed to stop."

He was lying, but I didn't know how to force him to cough up the truth. My hands balled at my sides.

He'd given us the story he wanted us to hear, and now he was shutting down, refusing to admit to anything else. He didn't want to compromise his boss's real decisions and secrets, after all.

Beckett flicked off the safety on his gun while leaving it pointed at the floor. "I'm going to need to hear a little more than that."

"Well, that's too bad, because that's all I have to say."

Lindell stared back at us as immovable as a statue, and my heart started to sink. He didn't look like a man who'd break under pressure. He obviously didn't shy away from the possibility of violence. What good did it do us if we battered him and broke his bones and still didn't get any answers?

He had way stronger motivation to stay quiet, didn't he? What would Doom's Seed do to him if he found out his lieutenant had confessed?

I touched Beckett's arm and caught his gaze. "Can I talk to you for a second?"

Beckett searched my eyes and motioned me toward the front room. He glanced at the Vigil guys. "Make sure he stays glued to that chair."

Slade saluted him, and Logan nodded grimly.

We walked into the smaller room, Beckett shutting the door firmly behind us. The faint growl of a car passing on the road outside filtered through the shaded window.

Beckett rested his hand on my shoulder. "What's going on, Maddie? Did you notice something you didn't want to mention in front of him?"

My mouth twisted. I spoke in a low voice to make sure it wouldn't travel to the other room. "I mean, I'm getting a strong impression that he's making a cover story for Doom's Seed and lying through his teeth, but that's not very helpful. It's starting to seem like he's not going to admit to anything. Even if you… hurt him, or whatever you'd normally do." I restrained a cringe.

A shadow crossed Beckett's expression. "I actually agree, Maddie," he said. "He wouldn't have risen to the level of responsibility he has under the boss he's got if he broke easily under pressure, and we don't have much time. Which is why I made sure I'd have an ace up my sleeve if I got a chance to hash things out with Lindell. I think it might be enough to crack him."

I raised my eyebrows. "What?"

"I'd rather—" He let out a rough breath. "I'm going to have to say some things that I would never actually act on. But he has to believe that I would. So I'm going to be convincing about it, and it isn't going to look pretty. I'm not going to tell you what you can handle, but I don't love the idea of you seeing me like that. Are you sure you're ready to witness how far I need to go sometimes to get the job done?"

My stomach lurched. "You want me to leave?"

"I'm not telling you to. I just want you to be prepared, if you do stay… and to know it might be better if you stepped outside and didn't have to hear it."

He paused, holding my gaze, and something in his expression softened. "Hell, if you told me it isn't worth it, that you don't want me to even pretend to be a monster, I'd listen to you. But it could mean we lose our chance at getting the answers we need."

I dragged in a breath, struggling to pull my whirling thoughts into order. Part of me recoiled at the thought of watching Beckett bring out the cruelest side of his criminal persona… but I knew that wasn't really him, didn't I? If he said he'd never act on what he was going to say, then I believed him. I knew he walked a difficult line doing his best to avoid unnecessary pain.

Being scary was part of how he got important things done—and this was the most important situation I'd ever faced. I had to be able to face every side of him, or how could I be with him? With any of the guys, really, considering they'd all gone to extreme lengths to see justice done in the past?

"I can handle it," I whispered. "Do what you need to do, and I'll be right here with you. I know what you stand for."

A sheen of gratitude and relief flickered in Beckett's eyes. He leaned in just for a second to claim a quick kiss.

"All right," he said. "Let's get this done."

He walked back into the room ahead of me. Lindell was in his chair where we'd left him, the Vigil guys poised around him. They eased back as Beckett came to a stop in front of the lieutenant. His face had hardened, and his voice came out icy cold.

"I think we've had enough of a run-around. You don't want to talk. I can understand that. But let's be clear: you need to give us something real, or you aren't the only one who'll pay."

Lindell snorted. "What are you talking about? Big talk from a little kid."

The smile that curved Beckett's lips was so chilling I had to tense my arms to stop from hugging myself. He leaned over the chair, setting his hands on its arms and pinning Lindell in place with his stare with just half a foot between them.

"A little kid," he repeated. "Interesting that you'd say that. Did you really think you could keep them hidden? I know about your girlfriend, Angela. I know about those cute little kids who should be thanking God they didn't end up with your ugly mug."

For the first time since we'd confronted him by the office building, Lindell looked shaken. The color drained from his face. "Fuck you."

"I really don't think that's how you should be talking to me." Beckett got out his phone and tapped on the screen. "Especially when I have people watching that lovely family of yours right now."

He held up the phone. Video played on the screen: a suburban backyard, a woman watching two kids race around on the lawn. A childish shriek of excitement reached my ears. My gut started to churn.

He wouldn't really do this. He'd told me that. But watching him now, I could see why he'd warned me. He *was* putting on the face of a monster.

"See the time stamp?" Beckett said in the same cold, even tone. "That's live. My men are ready to move as soon as I say the word. How many will it take before you remember the real answers to my questions? Should I have them start with little Benny, or maybe you're more attached to Delia?"

"Fuck *you*!" Lindell spat out again, jerking at his bindings. "If you touch one hair on their heads—"

"You're going to do what? You're tied up here. All you'll be able to do is watch. You know who you're dealing with, don't you, Clarence? I sit at the table alongside the man you call your boss. Would *he* hesitate to off a couple of kids if it got him what he wanted?"

From Lindell's sickened expression, Doom's Seed wouldn't. But he managed to sputter one more bit of defiance. "If you go after them, he'll know. He'll get payback—you'll regret everything ten times over."

Beckett shut off the video feed. "I wouldn't be so sure about that. You have a choice to make now, and you need to make it fast. You can keep your mouth shut, and then I'll kill you *and* your family and make sure word is passed on to Doom's Seed that we found out about this place we're standing in from you. Everyone will believe you're a traitor and that you got what was coming to you."

I hadn't thought Lindell could get any paler, but now he looked like a ghost. He opened his mouth, but he couldn't seem to find another argument.

"Or," Beckett went on, "you can tell us what we want to know, and your kids and their mother will continue living their happy, carefree lives. It's up to you. Like I said, we can always start with a half measure. Kill one kid, see if that motivates you to save the other. I'll make sure to have my men tell them exactly why they've come before—"

"Okay," Lindell broke in raggedly. "Okay. Leave them alone."

Beckett folded his arms over his chest and waited in silence. My throat constricted as Lindell took a few shaky breaths. But at least this was almost over.

"There's nothing all that complicated about it," he said finally. "That Evan Silver guy was poking his nose where it didn't belong, digging into the boss's businesses. So we arranged to have him taken out."

"Doom's Seed gave that order himself?"

Lindell shook his head. "I did. That was right after I was put in charge of this part of his territory. I'm not sure if he even knew about it—I didn't bother him with details like that. Silver hadn't gotten far enough into anything to cause any major problems."

"What was he looking for?" I had to ask. "Why was he poking around in the first place?"

"I don't know," Lindell said with a hopeless grimace. "I have no idea what he was searching for. I was just protecting the empire like it's my job to do."

"You have no idea at all?" Logan said, taking a step forward. "How about telling us how the specific businesses he was digging into were connected? What is *this* place?"

Lindell sighed. "There is no big connection that I

know about. We ship all kinds of stuff. This is one hand-off point to obscure the trail. All kinds of things have been moved through this space at different times."

Dexter frowned. "You came down on us awfully hard for someone who didn't think there was anything much to hide."

Lindell focused on him for a moment. "I came down hard on you kids because I thought you might have found something incriminating about any of our activities that I hadn't realized Silver had stumbled on. I was protecting my own. That's all there is to it."

My heart sank, leaving me feeling hollowed out inside. Could that really be it? There was no huge conspiracy—maybe even Dad had been wrong to imagine there was? He'd gone following a lead into the wrong place and been murdered because of it?

My voice came out thin. "You're telling me that you had my dad killed just for looking around a couple of buildings?"

Lindell just gave me a baleful look. "I don't know what else to tell you. That's just how things work in this business."

CHAPTER
TWENTY-FIVE

Logan

As I watched Doom's Seed's lieutenant answer Beckett's questions, the uncomfortable sense crept over me that none of this was really adding up.

Why would Maddie's father have been investigating standard criminal activities? It wasn't as if he'd been some kind of law enforcement. What would even have drawn his attention to a random crime?

But if there was something more to it, something unusual that did connect to his medical work, Lindell should have known that. And he was refusing to admit it.

I didn't see why Lindell would have gone to such lengths to make Evan Silver's death look like an illness either. That would have been difficult to pull off. Why not just shoot him and make it look like a mugging?

And the most important question of all: was the guy in front of us really responsible for Evan's murder, the mastermind behind everything we'd uncovered and faced during our investigation? Or was he still protecting his boss by taking all the blame?

I shifted my weight from one foot to the other restlessly, itching to grab Lindell by the front of his shirt and shake real answers out of him. But I could already tell that wouldn't get us any farther than we'd already gotten.

Beckett had come up with real leverage, enough for Lindell to confess to the parts of the story it was hardest to brush off. But now that he'd given us a full explanation that addressed all of our questions, how could we push him harder? I didn't want to start killing the guy's kids to see if he'd spill something else, and I doubted that Beckett did either.

His threat wasn't going to work as leverage any more if we weren't willing to act on it.

"What about the Baldwin file?" Slade asked, crossing his arms over his chest. "How does that fit into your boss's business?"

Lindell gave him a blank look that despite myself, I believed. "I don't know anything about that. Honestly."

That was totally possible. We only knew about it because of Evan's notes. It might have been something he'd seen at the hospital, something that hadn't actually been connected to Doom's Seed after all.

As the others continued to toss more questions at the lieutenant, I moved away, prowling through the strange room. Lindell had made it sound as if this place was only used for passing around deliveries, but the medical equipment was an odd choice. Was that just part of selling the front, or did they actually use it for some purpose he hadn't wanted to mention?

I moved through the area around the exam table, opening the cabinets and scanning the counters. There wasn't much in the storage space other than basic supplies like latex gloves, gauze, and antiseptic cleaner. Nothing that hinted at any specific activities.

I moved onward to the door Dexter had peeked through earlier. Stepping over the threshold, I flicked on the light.

There on the threshold, I paused to take in the scene that had come into focus in front of me. This was more than an exam room. It was obviously set up as an operating theater, with big circular lights mounted over a sturdy medical table, a sink in the corner, monitors off to the side connected to computer equipment too specialized for me to know what to do with.

A full row of cabinets lined the far wall, and a few smaller storage units stood around the electronic equipment. Everything was starkly white. The smell of the cleaner itched at my nose, bringing me back to the many hospital exams I'd endured since my own operation.

My skin prickled with apprehension. Why the hell would this nondescript, empty facility have a full-out operating room in it? Why would they have gone to this much trouble to stage the place if it wasn't being used? There were easier fronts they could have picked.

I pulled open the drawers on the storage units. At first I only found more of the basics, as well as sets of tools like scalpels and medical scissors. Then a drawer at the bottom slid out with a rattle to reveal several resealable plastic baggies full of pills.

My apprehension crept deeper into me with a chill that touched my bones. I pawed through the bags. They were unlabeled, but… I recognized the color and shape of a couple of them, along with the letters etched in their surface.

One of those types was the same kind I gulped down every day. The other I recognized was one I'd had in my regimen for years until the doctors had let me taper off. I could remember seeing it in the pill container Dad had made me use for organization, morning after morning.

What the hell was going on here?

Those medications could be used for other things, of course. One of them was a pretty standard antibiotic. I didn't recognize the other types of medication in the drawer.

Taking a page out of Dexter's book, I shoved down my growing uneasiness and snapped pictures of the bags with my phone so we could look them up later.

The cabinets at the back held medical gowns and face masks, more operating tools, and, crumpled in a corner behind other supplies as if it'd been accidentally forgotten there instead of getting thrown out, an empty bag with a label on the front. I tugged it out and smoothed the surface so I could read it.

Kidney Perfusion Solution.

The bottom dropped out of my stomach. For a second, I thought I might vomit. I dropped the bag and stepped away, the sharply sour smell of the place flooding my lungs.

Too many pieces were fitting together. Too much adding up… and making me wonder what else might be part of that equation.

I needed to get out of here, to clear my head and make sure I wasn't freaking myself out over nothing. I switched off the light and walked out, past the others to the entry room, right outside into the fresh air.

As the breeze washed over me, not really all that fresh with the whiffs of asphalt and car exhaust but better than inside, I let out a shaky breath. Dragged another in. Let it out again.

The things I'd found might mean nothing at all. They could all have been part of the staging. There could be legit operations happening in that place that had nothing to do with Doom's Seed or his illegal shipments.

But…

Before I had to follow that thought to its conclusion, the door opened. Maddie eased out and looked me over, her face tight with concern.

"Hey, are you okay?"

I opened my mouth and closed it again. I didn't know how to answer that question.

"I'm not sure. I—some of the stuff here—"

As I grappled with my words, Maddie touched my arm, her eyes softening. "Whatever's the matter, you can tell me about it."

I knew *that*. I knew how strong the woman standing next to me was. The problem was how much I wanted to admit to myself.

"The other room," I said finally. "It's set up like an operating theater. There were a bunch of pills—some of them the same kind I've taken since my transplant. And there was a bag of the stuff they use to store organs…"

My gut clenched up again with another jab of nausea. Maddie gripped my arm more firmly even as her eyes widened. "That is strange, but they have set this place up to look like a medical facility. They could have chosen to have those around for any number of reasons. Anyway, it has nothing to do with *you*."

She sounded so certain that I almost believed her. Almost.

I rubbed my hand over my hair. "I'm just getting a bad feeling that there's something worse going on than we've even started to suspect." Worse than I wanted to imagine.

Maddie held my gaze. "Whatever it is, we'll figure it out like we have so far. I think that—"

She cut herself off when a SUV pulled into the narrow lot a few spots farther down than Beckett's. Its glossy black shell held tinted windows that hid all view of the people within—until the back door swung open and a slim, blond woman in a posh dress-suit and sunglasses stepped out.

A sense of recognition hit me in that first glimpse, ricocheting through my brain. My mind was already starting to resist the idea rising up from my memories when the woman took off her sunglasses, and I couldn't deny it.

I was staring at my mom—what I had to imagine my mom would have looked like if she'd been alive for the past decade. Or else some mysterious identical twin I'd never known about. There were more lines at the corners of her eyes and lips and a few strands of gray in that golden-blond hair, but those dark eyes, that gently sloped nose, that hint of amusement in her quiet smile…

My heart had stopped. When the woman stepped toward me, it started beating again in a heavy, erratic rhythm. My throat closed up. I couldn't speak.

Her smile widened as she reached me. "Logan," she said with so much familiar warmth that the back of my eyes started to burn. That was her voice too, smooth and crisp.

She reached out to pat my shoulder, and I registered as if from a great distance away that the hand she'd pressed against me wasn't real flesh. She had a prosthetic attached to her forearm, the false skin a slightly artificial peachy shade that didn't quite match the rest.

On her left arm. Her left hand—the hand we'd buried in Mom's coffin because it was the only part of her remains we'd been able to recover after the gas main explosion.

Maddie had gone still beside me—how much because she could recognize Mom too from the few pictures she'd seen and how much because of *my* reaction to this woman, I had no idea.

My voice came out in a croak. "Mom?" And Maddie stiffened even more.

My thoughts were spinning in circles. This couldn't be possible. None of this made sense. How could my mother be *alive*? Where had she been all this time?

"I'm so proud of you, Logan," Mom said, beaming at me. "Seeing how determined and clever you've become has been amazing to watch. But this game needs to end here."

Before I could process those words, her expression darkened. Her prosthetic hand whipped from me to Maddie, the fingers closing hard around Maddie's wrist. She yanked Maddie toward her—and pulled out a pistol with her regular hand, pointing the muzzle right at Maddie's forehead.

A choked sound burst out of Maddie. "What are you—"

"Quiet," my mother said sharply, rapping the muzzle of the gun against Maddie's temple. My arm had been rising to reach for her, but both Maddie and I froze at that gesture.

"Mom," I rasped. "You can't—"

She gave me a firm look that was so familiar from my childhood I could have drowned in it. "Leave everything you've been digging into alone and go back to your normal life, starting now. Bring your friends with you. If you don't, *she's* the one who's going to regret it the most."

Without another word, she hauled Maddie back to the SUV and through the door she'd left open. Shock blanked my mind. Only as she yanked the door shut with a thud did I convince my body to spring into motion.

"Mom!" I yelled, lunging at the vehicle. It was already roaring out of the parking lot onto the road. My hand snatched at empty air.

No. *No.* This couldn't be happening.

But it was, and I couldn't stop it alone.

"Slade!" I screamed out as I dashed down to the road. "Dexter! Beckett! Get out here."

My world had just shattered into pieces, and I knew only one thing for sure. It wasn't going to be right again until the four of us got Maddie back from wherever the hell my mother meant to take her.

ABOUT THE AUTHORS

Eva Chance is a pen name for contemporary romance written by Amazon top 100 bestselling author Eva Chase. If you love gritty romance, dominant men, and fierce women who never have to choose, look no further.

Eva lives in Canada with her family. She loves stories both swoony and supernatural, and strong women and the men who appreciate them.

Connect with Eva online:
www.evachase.com
eva@evachase.com

Harlow King is a long-time fan of all things dark, edgy, and steamy. She can't wait to share her contemporary reverse harem stories.